SPIRIT ANIMALS™

FIRE AND ICE

SPIRIT ANIMALS™

FIRE AND ICE

Shannon Hale

SCHOLASTIC INC.

Arctica
Greenhaven Castle
Concorba
AMAYA
N

ERDAS
ZHONG
Jano
Rion
Xin Kao Dai
Shar
Liwao
OCEANUS
Hundred
Isles
Stetriol

For my brother Jeff, who once told me his spirit animal was a hippopotamus
–S.H.

Library of Congress Control Number: 2014933407

ISBN : 978-93-5103-548-0

10 9 8 7 6 5 4 3 2 1 14 15 16 17 18

Map illustration by Michael Walton
Conqueror dummy art by Erika Scipione
Book design by Charice Silverman

First edition, July 2014

Reprinted : Oct. 2014

Printed at Batra Art Press, New Delhi

Scholastic US: 557 Broadway • New York, NY 10012
Scholastic Canada: 604 King Street West • Toronto, ON M5V 1E1
Scholastic New Zealand Limited: Private Bag 94407 • Greenmount, Manukau 2141
Scholastic UK Ltd.: Euston House • 24 Eversholt Street • London NW1 1DB

1

GERATHON

GERATHON MOVED. HER BLACK SCALES, THICK AS PLATE metal, clicked against the sandstone. Her mouth was open, tasting the air. Her tail flicked playfully behind her.

Life! She thrilled with life, with her own body sliding over earth, and the earth sliding under her. Life is a pulse, a twitch, a flutter, an inhale. Life is movement. She wagged her tongue and tasted human on the breeze. More life! She wasn't hungry at the moment. Flocks of animals skittered, lumbered, and scampered after her, trembling with fear yet unable to turn away. Anytime she wanted a snack, she simply extended her great neck and snatched up a kangaroo or wild dog. She had not known hunger since her escape. All the same, life filled her with the desire to grab pulsing things and squeeze.

She changed directions toward the lone human, her weaving body frisky. She could move nearly silently, of course, but there was no need. What creature could outrun two tons of cobra?

This creature did try – a young man, his face still full of childhood when he looked back at her with wide-eyed fear. She hissed, a happy kind of giggle, and buzzed with the strength of her muscles and long, strong body. She spread the elegant hood of skin on her neck, coiled, and sprang.

Life! This life between her jaws thrashed, kicked, his heartbeat galloping against her tongue. He screamed heartily as her fangs pressed into his back, and her thick, black venom oozed inside him. His heart graciously pumped the venom along with his own blood throughout his body. He twitched for a time before going limp. But his heart was still beating, slow and lovely, as she swallowed him whole, her fantastic muscles pulling him foot by foot through her soft pink mouth into the final darkness of her belly.

She curled up and rested in the hot coral sands, enjoying the sensation of that second heartbeat beside her own, another life inside her, slowly dying by her own power.

She laughed now to remember how she had raged and seethed for centuries beneath her prison of rocks and dirt, the weight trying to crush life, swallow movement, end her. But new freedom made everything more delicious. Warm with sunlight and fresh food, she felt giddy and just a bit mischievous. She couldn't possibly eat another thing, yet her hunger for life was only piqued.

Her yellow eyes turned white as she reached out with her mind. Many white spots of heat vibrated behind her eyes, each one representing a person, all known to Gerathon as a shepherd knows her sheep.

Gerathon chose a sleeper. Easier to slip into the unconscious ones. This was a woman, elderly by human standards, living far away in Nilo. Gerathon's consciousness filled the woman's mind like sand fills a jar. She made her stand, leave her little house, and look around. Night in Nilo was brown and warm, scented with jasmine. Gerathon could almost feel the crack of dry grass beneath the woman's bare feet, the soil still holding heat from that day's sun.

Through the woman's eyes, Gerathon saw a cliff ahead. She moved her toward it, faster, faster, running now.

The woman flinched then, as if trying to wake up. Gerathon hissed pleasantly. Life is movement.

She moved the woman over the edge and fell with her, abandoning the woman's consciousness a moment before she hit the canyon floor.

A waste perhaps, considering Gerathon's plans for the future. But she needed to collect all the talismans first anyway, and in the meantime, a Great Beast deserves to play.

She licked the wind. The curl of her scaly mouth was always smiling.

2

THEFT

THE WIND WAS BLOWING FROM THE SOUTH, PUSHING AGAINST Meilin's back, urging her on. Not that she needed any urging. Lately fire seemed to rage inside her, flaring and snapping, insisting she move forward. The others sometimes complained about the endless travel and relentless pace through Zhong and now Northern Eura, but in Meilin's opinion, they couldn't move quickly enough.

Sunlight flared against the roadside river, and Meilin squeezed her eyes shut. As always, the same images were waiting for her behind her eyelids:

The Great Crocodile, jaws open, eyes deepest black.

Her father still. Gone.

Meilin quickly opened her eyes and heeled her horse into a faster trot.

The wind shifted. A breeze from the northwest rolled over her face. She rubbed the goose bumps prickling on her arms.

"It's going to get a lot colder," Rollan said, trotting his horse up beside her. "Unfriendly cold. Bite-your-nose-off-and-bully-your-toes cold."

"Yes," she said.

"I once saw a fellow lousy, good-for-nothing street kid dare a rich kid to lick an iron lamppost in the dead of winter. The rich kid's tongue stuck there – just frozen stuck – while the street kid robbed him of his coat and shoes."

"You don't say," said Meilin.

"Ah, but I do say, my lady panda!"

"And I don't suppose the street kid in your story had a name that begins with *R* and ends with *n*?"

"Certainly not! *I* was never lousy. And I only tell you this story as a warning because, you know, you do have that unfortunate habit of licking lampposts."

Meilin almost smiled. Ever since the battle at Dinesh's temple, Rollan had spent a lot of time near her, saying ridiculous things more often than not. Trying to distract her from her grief, she assumed. Their journey for the Great Elephant's talisman had been the most costly one yet. Striking out alone, Meilin had finally found her father leading an embattled resistance from within Zhong's Great Bamboo Maze. Then, almost as soon as she'd found him, he was gone – killed before her very eyes. At first Meilin had felt . . . quiet. Numb. It was an awful emptiness, like she had nothing left to give. But then, slowly, a heat began to kindle. A fire burned inside her, reminding her that somewhere the Devourer was free – and killing. Meilin wouldn't let sympathy or silly jokes put this fire out. She kicked her horse even faster.

"Crossroads ahead," Tarik announced. "Let's stop for the night."

"But there's still a little daylight left," said Meilin.

"The river veers away from our path at the crossroads," said Tarik. "We need to water the horses before we continue on north."

Meilin wanted to complain, but Tarik was looking at her again with understanding and sympathy. Jhi often gave her the same understanding and sympathetic look – which was why she kept Jhi in passive state as often as possible. It was becoming unbearable. The next person who looked at her with understanding and sympathy was going to get –

"Meilin?" said Abeke.

"What?" Meilin snapped.

"Oh!" said Abeke, starting back. "Um, I was just going to ask you if you wanted to help me gather firewood –"

"Yes, I do," Meilin said forcefully.

The flat ground around the crossroads was filling up, travelers and trader caravans setting up camp for the night. Their team was traveling up a flat, grassy expanse of Northern Eura. It was nowhere near Glengavin, sadly, or Finn, but the road was quiet and safe for once. There was even a minstrel troupe – a lute player strumming, a woman in a blue veil singing softly as if rehearsing.

Abeke didn't talk as they scavenged driftwood and broken branches from the riverbank. Good. Silence allowed Meilin to focus entirely on the burning inside, her whole being tuned to the idea of the Devourer, as if she were an arrowpoint and he the target.

With armloads of wood, they headed to where Tarik,

Rollan, and Conor were unsaddling the horses. Laying stones into a circle for the fire pit was the ginger-haired Euran Greencloak Maya, whom Tarik had asked to join them on their quest back to the North. She was older than Meilin by a handful of years, but her small pale face beneath her abundant curly red hair could be mistaken for someone younger.

Maya pushed up the sleeve of her purple sweater, exposing a small lizard-shaped tattoo on her forearm. With a burst of light, her fire salamander emerged from passive state and scurried up her shoulder. The black salamander bore bright yellow spots all over its body and was small enough to curl up in her palm. Meilin smiled sadly at Maya, certain the girl had been disappointed in her spirit animal, as Meilin had been with her panda. A salamander couldn't possibly lend any useful talents in battle.

Meilin and Abeke unloaded their wood, Abeke dumping some into the fire pit. Meilin was about to correct her. To start a fire, they needed smaller pieces of kindling first, and then –

Maya lifted her hand, and a ball of fire formed above her palm. She blew, and the fire shot into the wood, seizing the whole bundle in instant flames.

"Oh!" said Meilin.

"Hadn't you seen Maya's trick before?" asked Conor.

Meilin shook her head.

"I'm not much of a fighter, I'm afraid," said Maya with a generous smile. "I've got the one trick and that's about all I'm good for."

"That one trick might be indispensable for us in the icy North," said Tarik.

The veiled singer paced by; she and her lute-playing partner were on their way to the water. "You're heading north?" she asked. "Whatever for? Nothing is north of here but cold, more cold, and then really, really cold."

"And walruses," said Rollan. "I'm determined to see a walrus. If they're actually real."

"Rollan, I've told you," said Tarik, "I've seen them with my own eyes."

"Finned, legless elephants?" said Rollan. "I'll believe it when I see it."

"We're headed to Samis," Abeke said to the minstrels. "Have you been there?"

"Oh, Samis, that's right," said the lute player. "I'd almost forgotten there was any town between here and Arctica. No one bothers to go to Samis."

"We tried once, years ago, didn't we, my love?" said the veiled woman, holding her partner's hand and twirling around him. "Traders warned us that Samis turns away all visitors. But surely they're starved for entertainment, we said. So up we rode . . ."

"And, can you guess?" said the lute player. "Turned away at the town gate." He played a chord on his lute as if announcing the end of a song.

The pair danced off.

"No traders?" said Abeke. Uraza lay beside her, stretched out, and Abeke petted the leopard thoughtfully, evoking a bone-rattling purr. "In my village, without traders, we'd have no metal goods – no pots and pans, shovels, anything like that. If we purchase some metal items here to give to the people of Samis, maybe we can get in their good graces."

Tarik nodded. "A fine idea."

He removed a few coins from his purse and gave them to Abeke. She left to shop for the gifts, Uraza padding behind her.

A few minutes later Meilin heard angry shouts from across the camp. She stood, lifting her arm to call out Jhi, but resisted the urge.

"Are Abeke and Uraza still out there?" Meilin asked.

"Stay here," said Tarik, running toward the noise.

But that fire was burning in Meilin, and she couldn't sit still. She raced after Tarik, Rollan following, leaving Conor and Maya to tend the fire and watch their things.

In the center of camp, two men rolled around in the dirt, throwing punches and yanking hair. Tarik's spirit animal, the otter Lumeo, rode on his shoulder. With his abilities enhanced, Tarik dove into the fight as easily as an otter into water and separated the men.

"Enough!" Tarik said, and the catcalls and shouts died out. "What's going on here?"

"He robbed me!" The speaker was a stout, bald man. His nose was bleeding, his shirt torn. "I'd been saving up for years now, a coin here, a coin there. I almost had enough to take home, get my mother out of that dirty city, buy her a farm in the country. Almost had it! Till he cut the purse from my belt."

He lifted the corner of his shirt, showing the cut ends of two leather straps still tied to his belt.

"I'm telling you, it wasn't me!" said the other. "Bill, I've traveled with you for years. Why would I rob you now?"

"I don't know! But you're the only one I told about it, and if you didn't take it, where'd it go?" said Bill. He sat back in the dirt, crying into his hands. "I saved for so long. . . ."

"Sir, your friend is telling the truth," said Rollan. "He didn't rob you."

Meilin glanced at Rollan. Essix was circling the sky nearby. In the past, she had to be touching Rollan to enhance his intuition. Perhaps the bond between the boy and his gyrfalcon was improving at last, though Meilin had still never seen Essix take the passive form.

The one called Bill looked up, his dirty face streaked with despair. "Then who did?"

Rollan scanned the crowd of traders, musicians, and travelers who had gathered to watch the fight. A curious hush fell over the group.

Rollan's eyes stopped on one lanky young man wearing a crisp white shirt and cravat, who was inspecting a wagon wheel, his back to the fight. Rollan's brows narrowed.

"I'd check fancypants over there," said Rollan, nodding in the man's direction.

Tarik grabbed the lanky man's arms, holding them behind his back.

"What are you doing?" Fancypants shouted.

"I mean, that is a *stunning* wagon wheel," said Rollan, "but maybe not quite fascinating enough to pull your attention from a camp brawl? Unless you're just trying not to be noticed."

Meilin and another trader patted him down. Meilin felt a bulge in his boot and reached in, pulling out a leather sack heavy with coins, its strings cut. She tossed the bag to Rollan.

The man struggled, cursing. Meilin stood, her hands in eager fists. That fire inside her flared, threatening to burn her if she did not strike a blow, take down the Devourer and all his followers. Perhaps this petty thief would do for now. But Tarik held him tight, and Meilin exhaled, letting her fists relax.

Rollan held the bag up to the man's cut strings.

"That looks like a match to me," said Rollan.

Rollan handed Bill the purse.

"Thank you," Bill whispered, clutching it to his chest.

"At the last crossroads someone was robbed too," said an older woman with pulled-back white hair and rough riding clothes. "That was you as well, wasn't it, Jarack?"

The man called Jarack just thrashed in Tarik's iron grip.

"Traders have a code!" said the woman. "You broke it. Jarack, you are banished from this caravan and from ever trading in the North."

Jarack looked as if he would speak, but a dozen traders moved in behind the woman, some with folded arms, some bearing weapons. Tarik let him go. Jarack cursed, grabbed a pack from his wagon, and ran off into the night.

When Meilin and Rollan walked back to camp, Bill and his friend were shaking hands.

"Nothing like a robbery and caravan scuffle to get you warmed up for supper," said Rollan.

Meilin slowed her steps so she could walk beside him. She opened her mouth, readying a retort, something that might make Rollan laugh or fire back, start a conversation that would keep them talking for hours. But instead of words in her throat, she felt only searing heat – anxious, needy. She picked up the pace, leaving him behind as she neared their camp.

Up ahead, she saw Conor, lying back against his wolf, Briggan, petting his head. Maya was on her stomach, holding her fire salamander, Tini, on her palm and talking earnestly.

All Greencloaks spoke to their spirit animals, but Maya was holding what appeared to be an intense one-sided conversation with an amphibian! Perhaps she was mad, but she seemed so content, at ease. Everything Meilin was not.

Perhaps Jhi could help . . . *no*. Meilin clenched her fists, refusing the thought. Jhi *would* calm her down. But Meilin didn't want peace. She wanted a fight! The rage in her flared hotter, scalding her chest, her throat. She pressed her eyes shut to keep from crying and saw the image again: *Her father, still, his eyes vacant.*

A sob hit her throat like a fist. She opened her eyes and released Jhi.

The panda landed on the ground, turned, and looked at her. As always, Meilin thought the panda looked comical, black limbs over a white body like ill-fitting clothes, the black rings around her eyes drooped down as if sad. Everything about the beast was round and cuddly. Meilin wanted to be angry yet again that she hadn't bonded with a predator, fierce and battle ready.

But Jhi's silver eyes stared at her, intent. Meilin returned the gaze, took a breath, and suddenly everything seemed to slow.

Meilin became aware of the cool breeze against the

hairs of her arms, of the rich, velvety blue of the evening sky. Sounds seemed to break apart, and she could easily separate voices from the rushing of the river – the many conversations at camp pulling apart into their own pieces, the footfalls from Rollan coming up behind her, and just beyond him, faster footfalls. Running.

She turned. Time wasn't really slowed. Wrapped in Jhi's peace, her perception of the moment was so intense the world just seemed slow.

Rollan smiled at her. "What?" he asked.

He couldn't see. Jarack was running at Rollan's back, and he was holding a long, curved knife.

"Rollan!" Meilin shouted.

The calm from Jhi still surrounded her. Before Rollan even had a chance to turn and look, Meilin noticed a rock by her foot, kicked it into her hand, and threw, striking Jarack in the shoulder.

Startled, Rollan took a step back, inches from Jarack's knife. By then Meilin was already in motion, running forward. She slid the rest of the way, knocking her feet into Jarack's legs, sending him off balance. She could see from the way he moved that he had no martial training – but he had plenty of rage and a very large knife. He wasn't going to give up.

He swiped. Meilin seemed to see the arc of the knife's trajectory as if it were drawn in the air, slowly nearing her neck. She dodged easily, leaning to deliver a kidney punch. Jarack doubled over and then swiped again. This time she punched his sternum, knocking the wind from him, then made a sharp cut with the edge of her hand against his arm. He dropped the knife. Holding his wrist, he looked at her, eyes afraid. He turned and ran away.

Rollan was staring at her with absolute surprise. The wave of calm emanating from Jhi dissipated, and time seemed to click forward again at its natural pace.

"You were moving so fast," he said. "How did you do that?"

"I didn't feel fast," she said. "Everything else just seemed slow."

Rollan frowned.

"I'm sorry, Rollan," said Meilin. "You probably think I'm bossy and pushy, and you could have handled him yourself, and I shouldn't interfere all the time and –"

"Meilin!" he said. She realized he'd been saying her name over and over. "Meilin, thank you."

"You're welcome," she said and started to turn.

"No, I mean it." Rollan hesitated. "I . . . on the streets, I was always part of a crew, but if one of my crew had to choose between me and a hot meal, well, I knew which way he'd go. But here with you . . . you guys, for the first time . . . I guess what I'm trying to say is, I trust you. And for me, that's a big deal."

He smiled that Rollan smile that she was coming to know so well. At first he'd just been some orphan boy to her. And now here she was standing before him, an orphan herself – mother dead birthing her, father killed by the Devourer – homeless, nowhere to return to, just trying to survive. More like him than she'd ever imagined possible. His brown eyes were warm, his brown skin speckled with dirt from the road, his broad face comfortingly familiar. Inside the great void of despair that had filled her since her father's death, she felt a pinprick of hope.

And then Rollan reached out and took her hand. His fingers were warm.

Meilin had never been so aware of the beating of her heart.

3

SAMIS

THE ROAD TO SAMIS BEGAN TO LOSE ITS ROADNESS. GRASSES and brambles reclaimed the hard dirt, and Conor was confident they were actually headed somewhere only because Tarik had a map to follow.

Before he saw any sign of the village, Conor spotted a herd of caribou. The gray-coated, big-antlered animals grazed a green countryside, watched over by two –

"Shepherds!" said Conor. "Or caribou herders anyway. I'd like to go talk to them."

"Sure," said Rollan. "Have at it. Just, you know, don't give them the Slate Elephant or Granite Ram. I mean, if you can help it."

"Rollan," Tarik said quietly.

Rollan shrugged, unconcerned at the rebuke.

Conor felt sick. He'd been foolish to hope that the others had forgotten how he'd given the Iron Boar Talisman over to the enemy in exchange for the safety of his family. Not forgotten or forgiven.

Conor pretended not to hear and just walked on.

Two young men were sitting on the grass, chatting in the shade of a lone tree in a patch of pink and lavender lupines.

Conor carried a shepherd's crook with him on this journey back in Eura. He knew it would likely serve little purpose beyond a walking stick, as there had been precious few sheep to herd on their quests. But the thick wood staff felt right in his fist, its heft as familiar as the smell of woodsmoke in the hearth at home, the pinesap crackling, his mother's bread baking. After the frightening battle in Zhong and the whole Iron Boar business, a crook in his fist was comforting, even if it meant never using the crook for its intended purpose.

Now, though, he raised the staff high as he approached, hoping to greet the herders as colleagues. He expected a wave in return, maybe a hello. Perhaps an invitation to join their shade. Instead, they jumped to their feet, looking cautious. Both were blond and fair and looked to be twenty years old or nearly so. Their dark blue jackets and brown trousers seemed clean and unworn, perfectly fitting their broad, athletic builds. No herders Conor knew wore clothes so fine.

"Hello!" said Conor. "My name is Conor, and I'm a shepherd myself. Or I was until I joined up with my Greencloak companions there. My family kept sheep in central Eura. You're watching caribou? I've never seen a herd of domestic caribou before."

"We don't see visitors to Samis," said one.

"Never," said the other.

"We won't be staying long," said Conor. "Do you ever keep sheep, or just caribou?"

The herders glanced at each other but didn't answer.

Conor was aware of his teammates behind him, waiting for him to form some kind of herder bond with these strangers. He sighed at himself and kept at it. Though the herders rarely spoke a word, Conor went on about sheep, the different breeds, asking in-depth questions about caribou eating and sleeping habits.

While he was talking, Conor's practiced eye caught motion in the forest of firs that bordered the meadow. Shadow sliding over shadow, a glint of eyes.

"Is that . . ." Conor began, pointing.

The herders turned, squinting.

"Oh, no, they're back," said one.

The boys whistled, frantically calling to their herd. The caribou started and began to run away from the woods. The shadows emerged from the fir forest. Five brown wolves. The shaggy, lean beasts ran at the nearest caribou, splitting as if to meet it from all sides.

"Briggan!" said Conor, pulling up his sleeve. Pain briefly seared the back of his forearm, and the great gray wolf left passive state and leaped to the ground. "A pack over there. They'll hunt these people's caribou."

Briggan howled.

The wolf pack cut short. One howled back. Briggan responded. The wolves seemed to consider, then with a yip, the pack leader renewed the hunt, the rest following.

Briggan growled and ran. His speed both alarmed and thrilled Conor, as his wolf cut off the wolf pack before they reached the fleeing caribou. He launched himself at the pack leader, seizing him by the neck, the two rolling through the grass. They separated, both hunched low and growling, all teeth showing.

The rest of the pack was surrounding Briggan now – five to one. Conor began to run closer, his speed enhanced with Briggan in active state. His legs felt strong and long, the grass whipping by as he sped forward, clenching his crook. His heart pounded.

But before he reached them, the pack leader stopped growling. He circled as if chasing his tail, head down, nose nearly touching the ground. The submissive posture surprised Conor, coming from the leader of a pack facing just a lone wolf. Then again, that lone wolf was Briggan, one of the Four Fallen.

The pack leader howled and retreated to the forest, the pack following.

Briggan trotted over to Conor and accepted a hearty neck scratch and much petting.

"Good boy, Briggan," said Conor. "Thank you."

The herders approached, eyes wide.

"A wolf with blue eyes," said one. "He's Briggan, isn't he? *The* Briggan."

Conor nodded. And at last he wasn't the one doing all the talking. The herders had to recount to each other all the Briggan legends they knew. One took Conor by the arm and said, "Come on, Old Henner will want to hear about this."

Leaving the other with the herd, the young man ran with Conor toward the small gate in the village fence.

"Henner, you'll never guess!" the herder shouted at a man standing just inside the gate. "Briggan saved our caribou. *The* Briggan!"

And then he was retelling the whole incident, embellishing the more exciting bits.

Henner smiled through the gate's little window. "Briggan! You don't say? But what are you young folks doing up here?"

"We need to meet with your lord, or–" Conor looked over the village, considering it too small to have a lord like the duke in Trunswick. "Do you have a mayor? It's really important."

Tarik and the others came up behind him then. Henner looked them all over.

"Pia doesn't meet with visitors," he said.

"We have some gifts for Pia and your village," said Abeke, pulling two metal pots and three metal knives from her pack.

Henner's eyes widened again.

Conor noticed the buttons on the herder's jacket were cut from antler, as were the knife in his belt and the buckle itself. Even the hinges on the gate were made of leather. Cut off from traders, this town had a metal shortage.

"We also carry news," said Meilin. "We wish to warn your mayor and trade information. I think we can be of some help to you, and we will of course be at your service and depart the moment you ask."

Henner considered Meilin, the metal gifts in Abeke's hands, and Briggan beside Conor.

"Well . . ." Henner began.

"Oh, just let them in for a bit," said the herder. "We never have visitors, and you should have seen what Briggan did! *The* Briggan!"

Henner smiled and opened the gate. "I guess it couldn't hurt this once. Follow me."

"Well done," Tarik whispered just loud enough for Conor to hear.

"We don't trade much," Henner said, leading them up a narrow path. "Our villagers like to keep to themselves. A quiet people."

Loud laughter startled Conor.

"Not *that* quiet," Rollan muttered.

They were passing a small park area, abundant with lupines, tulips, and buttercups. On a bench built from wood slats and antlers, three young women sat, talking and laughing. They were as blond, tall, and athletic-looking as the herders had been. For that matter, so was Henner. For all his talk of "young folks," *Old* Henner couldn't have been more than a few years older than the herders. Conor wondered if they were all siblings.

A huge, ancient weeping willow bowed over a tiny cemetery.

"Look," Meilin whispered. "The stones have names – but not dates."

Conor nodded, though he didn't understand what Meilin meant. He'd never seen a cemetery before and didn't know why the absence of dates might be strange.

The dozens of houses looked nearly identical – long and narrow; gray stones cemented together for the foundation, the rest built from wood and painted red. The roofs were shingled with rough-cut bark, and the chimneys were built from fat and irregular stones. From house to house the only obvious variations were in the shutters and the doors on their leather hinges, each carved and intricately painted with unique designs of flowers, trees, woodlands, and often, a great white polar bear.

No road cut through the village, no sign of horses or wagon ruts. Paths were evenly spaced and marked with fine gravel, winding between houses and small parks. The village square was large and open, with a bright green lawn surrounded by stone paths and tulip beds.

Conor slowed, walking with the other three and letting Tarik and Maya keep pace with Henner.

"Those carvings are pretty," said Conor, indicating the shutters. "I can't imagine shepherds and farmers having time to sit and carve. Back home we kept busy just to stay fed."

"These folks seem to have all the time in the world," said Abeke, watching a couple strolling down a lane, holding hands.

"Could this be the lost city of chiseling artists?" asked Conor.

"Lost what?" said Rollan. "Chiseling who?"

"You know, from that song," said Conor, and he began to sing. "'Hidden from the ruinous wind, they chiseled a city from snow. . . .'"

"It's just a song," said Meilin. "You think all songs are real? In that case, I am excited to finally meet 'the jolly giraffalump what slurps pigs through its nose.'"

"Or remember this one? 'The giant tooted one horn with his mouth,'" sang Rollan, "'a second with his other end. And with both blasts, he amassed a crowd of admiring friends.'"

"I am unfamiliar with that particular song, Rollan," said Abeke. "Could you perhaps explain the 'other end' bit? I find it confusing."

"Well, it's . . ." Rollan paused, eyes scanning Abeke's

face as if to determine how serious she was. She gave him a faint smile.

"Anyway, it does look like a village for dolls," Meilin interjected. "The emperor's daughter had such toys. Tiny, perfect painted houses she set up for her tiny, perfect dolls."

"Exactly." Rollan looked around and began to whisper, "Even the people look . . . well, they look like dolls."

Apparently all the children and elderly were indoors, because everyone Conor had seen ranged in age from teenager to early adulthood. The men and women were all tall, with broad shoulders, strong arms, and lovely, perfect faces. Their hair color ranged from pale brown to gold, and everyone was smiling.

Conor shivered, remembering Trunswick – the darkness, the guards with mastiffs, the fear in the streets. Here everything was just the opposite – bright and perfect. And yet Samis too felt just a little bit off.

Briggan sniffed the air and sneezed.

4

PIA

ABEKE TRIED TO IMAGINE WHAT LIFE WOULD HAVE BEEN LIKE growing up in a place like Samis. So green! Leisure to plant gardens, stroll through parks, carve shutters. Even as a small child, Abeke had felt the crushing weight of need – need for rain, for meat, for crops to grow. Need to survive. No time for games or parks.

And beneath it all, the need to make her father and sister proud. That part still hadn't diminished. She gripped her bow and walked faster.

"Can we meet with your local Greencloak?" Tarik was asking Henner.

"Uh, well, we don't have one," said Henner. "Never really needed one."

Never needed one? Even in Abeke's small village, they'd had a Greencloak – someone with the Nectar, someone to conduct the bonding ceremony with the children when they turned eleven. It didn't matter if a child was in Eura or Nilo or anywhere – if that child was destined to bond with a spirit animal, it would happen with or without the Nectar. But without, the child could get the bonding sickness and risk madness or even death.

Abeke thought it unforgivably stupid of these villagers to risk their children by refusing to allow a Greencloak in the village.

Then again, where *were* all the children?

Henner stopped at a house where a woman was weeding a garden around peas and lettuce.

"Pia, we have some visitors," said Henner.

Pia stood up slowly. She appeared to be older than everyone else Abeke had seen in Samis, though her fair skin was unwrinkled, her dark blond hair free of gray. She wore a dark blue dress with a full skirt that stopped just below the knee. It was trimmed with bands of red and topped with a fringed yellow collar. The other villagers wore similar outfits cut from the same blue and red clothes, the same felt boots with curled-up toes, but only Pia wore the yellow collar. Abeke guessed it was some sign of her rank – like the epaulets on the shoulders of military leaders, or even her own green cloak.

"I see you've come a long way," said Pia. "But I'm sorry, Samis doesn't entertain visitors."

"That boy there has bonded with Briggan," said Henner. "He drove off the wolf pack that's been harassing the herd. And the Nilo girl brought us metal."

Abeke handed Pia the pots and knives. Pia looked over them as if at all the gold of Zhong, hefting them in her hands.

"This is . . . this is very kind. Thank you." Pia smiled. And with that simple gesture, Abeke didn't feel worried anymore. The strangeness of the town, the long journey, and the strained welcome all faded for her in the power of one genuine smile. Something in Abeke warned that she shouldn't be quite so trusting, but she just didn't believe bright smiles could hide dark hearts.

"If we could just speak with you a moment," said Tarik.

Pia pressed her lips together, but the smile returned and she gestured them inside.

The little parlor of her house was neat and clean – wood benches were topped with leather cushions, a carved table showed tiny animals whittled from bone. Several sets of caribou antlers hung on the walls, their tips filed down and fit with candles. Under their feet was a rug of woven fir roots.

They sat, and Meilin spoke first, as if she'd been holding in words she couldn't bear to keep quiet any longer.

"Zhong has fallen," she said.

Pia inhaled sharply.

"A new Devourer has risen, calling vast armies to his terrible cause," said Tarik. "If Zhong has fallen to the Conquerors, Eura won't be far behind. If Eura falls, Samis will fall with it."

"You came all this way to warn us? There are no soldiers here to help in your war," said Pia. "We are too small to –"

"We're looking for Suka," said Tarik.

There was a brief pause, and Pia turned so still and thoughtful that she seemed to have fallen asleep with her eyes open.

"She's a giant polar bear," Rollan prodded. "You know, from the stories? The stories that mention this village? That you are living in right now? No? Nothing?"

Pia's eyes darted to Rollan and back to Tarik, and then she laughed. "Suka! Well, she's not here at the moment, but I expect her to stop by for supper any minute." Pia laughed again.

An expression of measured disappointment clouded Tarik's face. Abeke hoped it wasn't a sign of bad things to come.

"Greencloak scholars uncovered several legends that say Suka showed favor to your town," said Tarik. "Supposedly the last place she was seen was here in Samis."

"Yes, I've heard the legends," said Pia. "But legends are old, and if Great Suka used to favor our town, she hasn't been to Samis in many, many lifetimes."

"She used to drink from a pond here," said Tarik. "May we see it?"

Pia hesitated, but then that wide smile returned. "Of course. It is sacred to us, so I'll ask you not to touch the waters. Follow me."

At the very north end of the village grew two ancient willows, their branches sheltering a pond. Perhaps the pond was natural, but people had placed stones around it, even lining the pond's bottom with smooth, flat rocks. The water was so clear, Abeke could see the stones easily through five or ten feet of water. The surface rippled as if stirred by a breeze, though Abeke felt nothing.

"This is Suka's pond," said Pia. "She . . . Legend says she used to come here once a year and drink."

"How could Suka get here when the village is walled in?" asked Rollan.

"You think that a little wall would slow down a Great

Beast?" asked Pia. "Besides, this was long ago, before the wall surrounding Samis was built."

She gestured to a carving of an upright polar bear, cut from a jagged white rock.

"We honor her with this memorial, but of course we have no idea where Suka has been hiding all these years."

"It seems weird to me that you would flat-out lie to us like that," said Rollan.

Pia started, then smoothed her features.

"*Rollan*," Abeke whispered. Maybe he'd never learned to respect his elders. If Abeke had dared talk like that to her father, she'd get switch whipped.

"That's an impertinent thing to say, young man," Pia said.

Rollan shrugged. "Sorry. Still true. You're hiding something."

Essix wasn't perched on Rollan's shoulder. Could Pia's lies be clear enough that Rollan could detect them even without his gyrfalcon in direct contact? Or perhaps his spirit-animal-enhanced intuition was getting stronger.

"You say Suka came before the wall was built," said Meilin. "Yet the layers of reindeer moss growing on the wood shows the wall's age, going back to even before the time of the Devourer, perhaps."

"I had a dream last night," said Conor. "I thought it was just a dream, not a *dream* dream, you know what I mean?"

Abeke nodded. Since bonding with Briggan, Conor sometimes had prophetic dreams.

"But I recognize this pond from my dream," Conor continued. "A group of elderly people was staggering along toward it, and their faces were eager."

Pia's pale face turned even paler.

Abeke had kept Uraza in passive state up till now so as not to seem hostile, but she needed her leopard's aid now. She reached a hand slowly toward the pond, palm up, almost as if the waters were a wayward puppy she was about to call toward her. In a quick motion she brought her fingers into a fist, and Uraza flashed into existence. Pia stumbled back a step, stunned at the appearance of yet another Great Beast, even though like Briggan, Uraza was the size of a normal leopard. Uraza padded toward the pond as if to drink.

"No one drinks from this water! Neither human nor beast, be it Great or common!" said Pia. "It is sacred!"

The leopard sniffed at the water and recoiled, looking back at Abeke, communicating that something was wrong.

"Don't worry, she doesn't want to." Abeke sat at the water's edge with a hand on Uraza, in part to reassure Pia, but also to feel some of the clarity of thought that came with their bond. There were pieces of something here, a fractured story that could fit together like the gazelle-antler puzzles that Chinwe, her village's Greencloak, used to carve. Abeke had always been good at those.

Rain Dancer. Chinwe had declared Abeke the new Rain Dancer for the village, but her bond with a Great Beast had forced her to leave. Now she allowed herself to soak in that title, to feel community with the water before her, sense it as she would the presence of a friend standing near, her hand stroking Uraza's neck. She was dimly aware of the conversation continuing without her, Tarik and Pia and Rollan speaking in turn. But Abeke pointed her thoughts instead to the water. To Pia. To the people of Samis. No children, no elders. Conor's dream. The gate and wall. *Old* Henner.

All the pieces of this puzzle were snapping together in Abeke's mind. She knew this story. In Nilo the legend was of a tree whose fruit would keep you young forever, and two villages that destroyed each other and the tree itself while trying to possess it.

A tense pause in the conversation seemed to vibrate the air around her, and she stood.

"You know," Abeke said, "it's interesting that there are no children or elderly in your village, Pia. And there's something different about this water that Suka used to drink. Uraza can smell it. And Conor's dream about elderly people hurrying toward the pond? I'm thinking that you're much older than you look, Pia. I'm thinking Old Henner might actually *be* old. You all are. And that has something to do with Suka's pond."

Rollan looked at the water, taking a step back. "That's unnatural."

"You can't think –" Pia began.

"Perhaps we should all drink from the pond," said Tarik. "Just to check Abeke's idea."

"Ooh, what do you think, Tini?" Maya asked her salamander, holding him in her palm. "Do you want to live forever and ever and ever and –"

"No, wait." Pia sighed, sitting on a rock beside the pond. She looked at each one of them in turn, directly in the eyes, as if checking for something. She sighed again. "Very well. Suka did come to this pond and drink, every year on New Year's Day. The villagers have always avoided the place, believing the event was sacred. When I was young, my mother told me that as long as we kept the waters clear for Suka, we would be under her protection. But I was always curious. I wanted to see the Great Polar Bear for myself. So when I became mayor, I built my house near her pond, and I watched her, year after year."

Pia's eyes became unfocused, as if watching a memory. "She was huge and terrifying, but you've never seen anything so beautiful. It was as if the moon itself had dipped down to drink from our waters. Suka didn't seem to mind my company. I kept quiet, just watched her until she'd sated herself and ambled away. Nearly three decades passed that way – she and I and our little ritual.

"Then, one year, she simply didn't come. I went to the pond. I watched and waited, but Suka never arrived. It felt wrong, a breaking of a tradition. So early that morning, just before the sunrise, I crouched down and drank from the pond myself, to complete the new year."

Pia paused.

"The waters changed you," said Tarik.

Pia nodded. "A stillness came over me. I seemed to feel the bones of my skeleton as if they burned, and the gentle heat worked through my muscles, my skin. I was a grandmother at that time, but I seemed to get younger. Ever since, these waters have kept us young. Some chose not to take the water and lived a normal life span. Others grew tired of their long lives and stopped drinking. They aged within a few years and then died peacefully. Those who drink never have children, and all who remain in

Samis today have drunk. We are the last of our clan."

"You think Suka drank from here for the same purpose?" asked Meilin.

Pia shook her head. "The water here used to be pale brown like the river nearby, but the longer Suka stayed away, the more clear, crystal, nearly blue it became. I heard rumors years ago come down from Arctica that Suka had frozen herself and her talisman deep within the ice. I believe that with her powers in suspension, her tie to this pond is granting it life-giving magic. If you find Suka and wake her, the powers of the water might go away. Then all of Samis would dwindle and die."

"It's a terrible risk," said Tarik, "but the future will be even more terrible if the Devourer wins. We need to find her."

"It doesn't matter. I know nothing that would help you." She glanced uneasily at Rollan and then away. "You may stay the night and then you must go. We have no inn, so you'll need to sleep in the stable. Visitors might discover the secret of the pond, as you have. If the secret gets out, people would come from all over. Wars would be raged over its waters."

"Of course," said Tarik. "We swear to keep your secret."

Abeke mumbled affirmation. Conor and Meilin both intoned "I so swear" at exactly the same time, startling each other a little.

"I can keep a secret," Maya said.

"What secret?" Rollan said.

Pia raised an eyebrow, and then nodded. She didn't seem consoled.

Pia gave them dinner at her house – thinly sliced caribou meat on flatbread with onions and turnips. The meal was close enough to one Abeke had often shared with her family that she desperately wished for the burning tang of a bhut jolokia pepper or one of the dried grass spices of Nilo. She lowered her emotions like a blade, trying to cut off all longing. Just yearning for the food of home had cracked open her heart, reminding her of her father's hands as he sanded sticks for arrows, of her sister's voice singing as she cooked. She missed them more than peppers and spices, but a twinge in her heart reminded her that they probably didn't miss her.

She closed her eyes, sealing the cracks inside, refocusing on Abeke in Northern Eura, Abeke the Greencloak, Abeke who might never return home again.

Uraza pressed her large head under Abeke's hand, rubbing against her palm. Abeke lowered her plate, letting the leopard finish up the caribou meat.

As they settled into the fresh grass strewn on the stable floor, Tarik spoke of traveling north tomorrow and trying their luck exploring Arctica on their own.

"Conor, perhaps you could have a perfectly timed prophetic dream tonight telling us where to go?" said Abeke.

"I'll do my best," said Conor. He smiled.

"So we're just rolling with the whole 'Suka froze herself' thing?" Rollan said. "I admit that Pia didn't seem like she was lying about that, but you guys are all like, 'Yeah, sure, that sounds about right.'"

"It does sound about right," Conor said, tossing a stick down the long, narrow barn for Briggan to fetch.

"But it's *weird*. Does no one else think that is weird?"

Rollan looked around the group. "That a bear would freeze herself? How would you even do that?"

"I know a dozen ways at least," Meilin said. "Wise men and women in Zhong freeze themselves regularly."

"Wh-what?" Rollan sputtered.

"It is much more comfortable to pass the sweltering summers encased in ice," Meilin said.

"Fah!" Rollan snorted, throwing up his arms.

Meilin smiled slightly, though Abeke noticed that the smile quickly disappeared.

"And here I thought you were able to tell when people were lying," Conor muttered, smirking.

"Whatever. In any case, Pia knows more about all this," said Rollan. "I still think she could help us."

"But we can't force her to," said Tarik.

"I could burn down her house or something," said Maya through a yawn.

Abeke sat up, staring.

Maya laughed. "Kidding! Kidding!" She settled into the grass cuttings and muttered, "I mean, I *could* burn down her house. But I won't. Tini and I don't like hurting anybody, do we, Tini? No, we don't, you adorable little sticky-footed genius."

Abeke woke in the morning to Uraza sneezing on bits of hay. She lay stretched out beside Abeke, her body longer than Abeke was tall. Abeke idly stroked her belly and heard Uraza purr. The earth tremor of her purr would be enough to wake up the others.

Sudden noises came in through the window. Shouts.

Anger. Sounds that didn't belong in the perfect doll village of Samis.

By the time Abeke was on her feet, the others were awake and rising. They hurried out to the village center.

First she noticed a hole in the wall. Something had punched through the logs, leaving a gaping hole large enough for a person to climb through.

And it appeared some persons had in fact climbed through.

"Shane!" said Abeke.

A group of five Conquerors stood before the hole, but Abeke's eyes didn't stray from Shane – blond, broad, his arms and face tanned from the Zhong sun. The sight of his smile awoke a thousand memories – their hours together training, laughing, whispering stories, standing at the ship's bow with the spray on their lips, the wind against their faces, feeling as if the whole world could be theirs. Until Shane, Abeke had never known how it felt to be with someone who liked her, who respected her, who even wanted her around.

Abeke could feel her companions around her bristling, hear them pull out weapons, but she walked over to Shane to shake his hand. He surprised her by meeting her halfway, his arms open. He gave her a warm hug.

"I missed you, Abeke," he whispered into her hair. "I'm so glad you're here."

Abeke shut her eyes, feeling the sting of tears.

"Back off!" Conor yelled. He pulled Abeke away and faced Shane, holding his crook, Briggan tense by his side. "Touch Abeke again and I'll knock you flat on your stink-stained Conqueror behind!"

Meilin was beside Conor, and she didn't waste time with words. She came forward, hands in fists. A tall Zhongese man stepped smoothly in front of Shane, and when Meilin struck, the man defended. She delivered a series of blows that the man blocked with his arms, finally striking her with the palm of his hand. She stumbled back.

Meilin released Jhi. The panda sat calmly behind her, investigating the grass, looking entirely unthreatening, but Meilin smiled, lifted her fists, and said to the man, "Let's try that again."

"No, Meilin, Conor, stop," said Abeke. She and Uraza put themselves in front of Shane.

"We didn't come to fight," said Shane. "Please. We just want to talk."

"Breaking our wall is not talking behavior," Old Henner called out.

"I apologize for that," said Shane. "My companions were overeager when you didn't open the gate for us. I'll fix it with my own hands, I swear."

"I'll fix *you* with my own hands," Meilin said through clenched teeth.

Abeke and Uraza didn't move.

"So much has happened, so many deaths on both our sides," said Shane, his voice warm, melting like butter over hot bread. "Before anyone else dies, let's talk, please."

Abeke looked over Shane's companions now. Besides the Zhongese man, the two impostors they'd last seen in Trunswick flanked him. The pale-haired Tahlia held her toad in both hands like an ugly ball she was ready to throw in some horrible game to which only she knew the rules. Ana was one step behind her, crouched next to her gila monster. She stroked it as one might pet a cat, but her dark eyes were locked on the Greencloaks, peering hatefully between two curtains of straight night-black hair.

To Shane's other side were two larger warrior-type men, one atop an ox, the other with a brown-eyed lynx weaving between his ankles. They looked vaguely familiar, as if Abeke had seen their faces among the ranks of the Conquerors before. But the Amayan woman beside them was a stranger. She had pale brown skin, dark eyes, and long, straight black hair. Her long travel dress was dark purple, embroidered with yellow and white along the sleeves and hem. On her shoulder sat a grave-looking raven. But what most caught Abeke's eye was a striking sadness in the woman's beautiful face.

"So, talk," said Tarik. "We're listening."

"Tarik," Meilin growled. Her knees were slightly bent, her hands in tight fists. "We know what they want and what they'll do to get it. Let's take them now."

"Meilin," said Tarik. "Come here, please."

Meilin hesitated but complied. Abeke joined her group, and the six of them huddled to talk quietly, Uraza and Briggan standing like sentries between them and the Conquerors, teeth bared.

Meilin and Conor glared at Abeke. She expected the same look of anger or mistrust from Rollan too, but he was strangely distracted, just staring over his shoulder at the Conquerors.

"We can't leave now," said Tarik. "While we wander north in search of Suka, Shane and his crew might persuade or bully the information out of Pia and beat us to the talisman."

"So we fight," said Meilin.

"I'm not confident we could beat that crew," said Tarik.

"I could beat Shane," said Conor. "I have no doubt. I dreamed about it."

"A prophetic dream?" Tarik asked.

Conor fidgeted. "Figure of speech," he said. "Not like a nighttime dream. Like a detailed mental exercise."

"You mean, you daydreamed it," said Meilin. "You imagined punching his face in over and over again."

"Pretty much," said Conor.

"Yeah, I've had that daydream too," Rollan muttered.

"Shane means no harm, I swear," said Abeke. "Look, he doesn't have his wolverine out. He almost always keeps his spirit animal in passive state when he meets us. A true sign that he doesn't want to fight."

"No harm?" said Meilin, eyes burning with rage. "This is the agent of the very being responsible for the destruction of my home and the death of my father. I count those things as great, unforgivable harm."

Abeke closed her eyes and then opened them slowly. "And that is terrible, unjust, and not easily forgiven. But also not Shane. He's different. He truly believes he's on the side of right, just as I did."

"He. Is. The. Enemy," said Meilin, as if talking to a small child.

"I know he works for the enemy," said Abeke. "But I believe that one day he might be able to see the Devourer for what he is."

"So your secret hope is that Shane will abandon everything he stands for and . . . and change his entire worldview?" asked Meilin.

"It is possible. After all, I did."

"Yes, and seeing you embrace the Devourer's errand boy has shown me just how deep your conversion runs."

Abeke winced.

"Enough," said Tarik, the beginnings of a frown creasing an already stern expression. "We will not let them tear this team apart. First we will listen, and then –"

There was a sudden blunt cracking sound, as of a fresh kill being struck by a hammer. Abeke looked up quickly to see Shane on one knee, nose bleeding. Meilin stood in a fighting pose several paces away, seemingly too far away to have accomplished such a feat, but Abeke had seen how fast Meilin could move.

"Meilin, no!" Abeke shouted. For a moment Abeke was again at the battle of Dinesh's temple, knee-deep in water, the air so humid it seemed to push into every pore and try to crawl down her throat. Conquerors swarming at them like ants over fallen bread. An enemy soldier chopping at her, his sword stopped short by Shane's curved saber. Saved by this boy who was supposed to be her enemy.

And now he stood there, his nose bleeding from Meilin's fist.

The rest of Shane's group was variously standing, shouting, or drawing steel.

"Come on!" shouted Meilin. "You are due much more than a mere taste of your own blood, so I will do my best to serve up a feast."

The ox charged Meilin, and she leaped, pushing off of its advancing skull even as the head reared up. She vaulted faster than seemed possible to Abeke's eyes, doing a full turn in midair and landing, heel first, in the face of the man who had until recently been riding the ox.

"ENOUGH!" shouted several voices, but none was the owner of the maddened ox, so it spun, frothing at the mouth, and renewed the charge.

Meilin readied herself to dodge the oncoming beast, but Abeke saw Jhi amble into the charging animal's path.

"Jhi!" Meilin yelled, her stance breaking.

Jhi turned her passive silver-eyed stare to Meilin. And then, the instant before impact, Jhi simply looked at the charging animal. Abeke's jaw dropped as the ox, instead of barreling into the panda, skidded to a halt, knelt, and began to lick Jhi's paw.

"Enough," Pia called out again. Abeke realized the other voices calling "enough" had been Tarik and Shane. Pia had arrived in the town square, that same smile plastered to her face, despite what had just happened. Abeke began to question the sincerity of the smile.

"There is no fighting in Samis," Pia announced.

"Pia," said Tarik, placing a calming hand on Meilin's shoulder. "You have more visitors, as I expected. If you speak to Shane here, I want to be present as well."

She nodded and walked away. Tarik and Shane followed. Abeke hoped Shane would look back, so she could mouth that she was sorry or smile encouragingly or something. But his head was bowed, his hand holding a rag to his bleeding nose.

"Abeke, Conor, keep an eye on –" Tarik nodded toward Tahlia and Ana, the two brutes, and the mysterious woman. "And on Meilin," he added.

Abeke nodded. She had every confidence her big cat could take down any of the other spirit animals. And after this business with Meilin, her own heart was thrumming, her muscles tense, all of her wishing for a fight. But fight whom? Shane's friends? Meilin? Maybe her own self.

She put a hand on Uraza's head and took a deep breath. She would try to keep the peace. For Shane's sake.

5

AIDANA

Essix was gone. Everyone stood in the village square, bristling with weapons and spirit animals, and Rollan felt so bare he might as well be naked. That was why his hands were shaking, that was why his mouth was dry, and why he'd refused to look at the woman with the raven. He wouldn't admit to himself any other reason.

When no one was looking his way, he slipped behind a house and began to circle the inner ring of the town's fence.

"Essix," he hissed. "Please, Essix. Come on."

He couldn't really blame her. Sticking around where people expected you to be led only to trouble. He'd learned the hard way on the streets of Concorba: Keep moving. You stay in one place, the bullies find you. Beat you up. Steal the scrap of blanket and heel of bread you've been hoarding. Almost kill you.

Rollan got it. He just wished Essix would hang around every once in a while, bolster his reputation a bit as a fierce warrior with a faithful spirit animal in tow. On the streets, if you looked harmless, you ate dirt.

"Essix," he whispered again. His voice shook, still addled by the encounter with Shane – and who he'd brought with him. It wasn't possible. He *knew* it wasn't possible. But she'd looked so much like . . . He shook his head, angry at himself for getting rattled by a familiar-looking face.

Rollan crept behind one of the ridiculously adorable houses with its perfectly carved and painted shutters. When he heard footsteps coming from the other direction, he expected to see one of those tall, muscular, golden-haired beauties that passed as villagers around here.

But it was her.

The woman's hair was as black as her raven's wings, straight and thick, falling down to her waist. Her eyes were dark and large, her skin the brown of the best kinds of bread, her face broad. His breath got tangled in his chest. Something is beautiful, he'd come to understand, if you want to look at it. And her face had for many years been the most beautiful thing in the world to him. And for years after, her face was the image he couldn't help looking for among the crowds of Concorba. Every day, all the time, for years and years, though his heart hurt at the pointlessness of it.

He'd finally given up years ago. Well and truly, given up looking for her, wondering about her, hoping for her. She was dead, he'd been so sure.

Now here – across an ocean and in a strange little village near the top of the world – to see that face again.

Not her, can't be her . . . he told himself.

But her hands raised, and he noticed they were shaking. She seemed to reach for him before hesitating, dropping again. She looked behind her and back again. Her eyes were wide, as if she couldn't look at him hard enough.

"Rollan," she whispered. "Is it really you?"

He nodded. His head was giddy. His legs felt comically shaky, like sacks of sand.

"Rollan," she said again.

Then she began to cry.

She sat on a stone, and he took the excuse to sit too, unsure if he could keep his feet. He could feel the warmth of her arm so near his own, and the realness of her shocked him. This was not some little boy's desperate daydream. She was here.

"My name is Aidana. But . . . I think you know who I am?" she asked.

He nodded, feeling dumb.

"I'm sorry," she said. "I'm so, so sorry. You know that, right? You know I wouldn't have left you if I could have . . . if I wasn't . . . if I didn't love you enough to leave?"

She hadn't wiped her tears, just left them to run down her cheeks, letting nothing get in the way of looking at him.

Rollan felt his heart ice. Once, back in Concorba, he'd come across a girl alone, sitting on the street, crying loudly. Everyone else ignored her, but he'd gone closer to see if he could help. That was when the rest of her crew had jumped out, struck him in the head, and stolen the two coins he'd earned after a day of begging. When the girl had run off, her crying had changed to laughter.

Instinctively, Rollan looked around, expecting the attack.

No one jumped out.

"Can I – I know nothing will make up for all you might have suffered, but will you allow me to explain?" Aidana asked.

He nodded again, because he really couldn't think of anything else to do.

She took a deep breath, and then the words poured out, as if she'd been holding them in for a long time.

"I didn't mean to – I didn't want to leave you. You believe me? I had no father, no family besides a mother who lived with a bottle in her hand. I turned eleven and never had a Nectar Ceremony. When I was fourteen, Wikerus came to me." She nodded toward her raven, who was perched above them on the branch of a tree. "We bonded without Nectar. I felt" – she pressed her hands against her head – "like I'd been ripped apart. My head, my gut, it was so painful. I think I spent days in a fever, and when I became aware again, my mother had gone, but Wikerus stayed. He always stays."

The raven turned his head, staring at Rollan with one round eye.

"I survived as best I could, battling the bonding sickness. I wasn't well. And by the time I became pregnant with you . . . Rollan, I tried." Her voice cracked. "You were so perfect! Such a perfect baby. And at times when I was holding you I felt almost normal. But other times . . ."

Her eyes went dark.

The only image Rollan carried with him from his early childhood was her face, her beautiful face, as if it'd been carved in a cameo and worn against his heart. But as she spoke, he had flashes – her face in a rage, screaming. A bottle thrown into an alley, the explosion of glass, shards flying, cutting into his cheeks. His mother flailing, punching at bricks, while he huddled on a step, frightened. Wandering down a street, alone and cold, searching and searching, and then finding her asleep on the stones. And then curling up tight beside her – to keep her warm, to keep himself warm, to assure himself she would stay close this time.

"Some days I wasn't sure who I was – who you were," she said. "One time you woke me, crying in the night. We were sleeping high up in the attic of an abandoned building, and in delirium I thought you were a rat attacking me. I grabbed you and I almost, I almost . . ." Her breath shuddered. "After that I knew I had to get you away from me before I did something horrible. So I took you to a big house near the center of town. I'd watched that family for some time. They had lots of children, and at night the windows were always bright, as if they had plenty of money for candles. So I figured they could afford to keep you. Maybe even love you."

Rollan wasn't sure what house she meant. He had no memory of the place.

Aidana swiped quickly at her tears while she talked. "First I washed your face. And your hands. And your tiny little feet. You . . . you didn't have shoes, but I wanted you to have clean feet, so your new family would know you were a good boy. And then . . . and then I kissed your cheeks and told you to be good and stay put till the nice family came for you, and I knocked on their door and I . . . I ran."

Rollan didn't realize he'd been crying till he felt a line of cold pull down his cheek. He touched it, and his fingertips came back wet.

"I waited across the street till I saw someone open the

door. I knew they'd take you in and take care of you. You were such a smart little boy, I felt sure they'd see that. So I fled. And . . . I don't remember a lot of the next years. I wasn't always in my right mind. But I survived, somehow. Wikerus could steal fruit from trees and bread cooling on windows. Even when I got really bad, Wikerus never left me. Though he bit me sometimes. Clawed at me. He had the bonding sickness too."

She brushed her fingers unconsciously across her cheek, and Rollan noticed a series of pale scars. He thumbed a clash of old scars on his wrist and wondered if Wikerus had caused those as well.

"I think I was dead – or nearly – when Zerif found me. He gave me the Bile to drink, and slowly the darkness left my mind. The Bile cured both of us of that awful sickness. He saved us, Rollan. He saved me and Wikerus. I owe him everything. So of course, I serve him now – serve both him and the Reptile King. He isn't the 'Devourer' you think he is. They're out in the world, looking for people like me who the Greencloaks didn't bother finding, didn't bother helping, curse them."

She looked Rollan over, as if noticing that he wasn't wearing a green cloak, and she smiled approvingly. Her smile faltered.

"Rollan, I wish you'd say something," she whispered.

Rollan licked his lips, trying to work moisture into his mouth. He said, "Ma?" His voice was a dry whisper.

She grabbed his hands, rubbing them as if to warm him up. The gesture was achingly familiar.

He was afraid to ask but did. "Once you were well, did you look for me?"

"Yes," she said, clearly relieved to say it. "Yes, I did. I

went back to that house, but it'd been sold and the new owners didn't know where the others had moved. I hoped your new family was living in the country now – with animals, perhaps, and clean air and lots of fresh food. Did you move to the country?"

What could he tell her? She'd seen someone open that door, but she'd left before seeing them shut it again in the face of a ragged little boy. He wondered how long he must have stayed on the doorstep of the big house, waiting for a family to come for him like she'd said. He wondered how long he'd wandered the streets looking for her before giving up and finding a hole to sleep in alone. Should he describe to her the long years of starvation and fear, abandonment, loneliness, of his doing almost anything just to survive and dreaming of a mother who'd held his head to her chest and let him fall asleep against her heartbeat? Or should he tell a kind lie to put her at peace?

He hadn't yet decided when her raven squawked – a jarring, unnaturally loud sound. Wikerus batted his wings and took to the air as Essix came swooping down.

Essix shrieked at the raven. The two birds met midair, feet forward, and clawed at each other.

"No!" said Aidana. "Leave him alone!"

"Essix!" Rollan cried.

The gyrfalcon flew past Rollan and returned again, shrieking as she tried to seize the raven with her talons. The raven fought back, croaking hideously.

"Essix, don't hurt him!"

Essix spun, taking again to the skies, as if to get as far away from Wikerus as possible.

"Essix?" said Aidana, blinking rapidly. "Of course. *You* were one of the children bonded to the Four Fallen."

"I'm sorry," said Rollan. "I don't know why she attacked."

"It's okay. Wikerus isn't hurt." Aidana took Rollan's hand in both of her own, pressing it with warmth. "I don't want anything to detract attention from our reunion."

Rollan smiled and wanted to be okay, but he felt uneasy. Essix had warned him all those months ago to flee from Zerif. Her instincts had been right then and dozens of times since. And the memory of Zerif, and of the Conquerors killing Meilin's father, was still as fresh as a bleeding wound.

He almost leaned in then, ducking his head under her chin as if he were still a little boy, to let her embrace him. But crammed into those few inches between them he felt the years of solitude on the streets, the Conquerors' trail of death, and even a fight between a raven and a falcon.

"I – I should go check with my . . . uh . . . team," he stammered and turned and left before he could change his mind. As he walked away, he felt a raw pang in his chest, as if a chunk of his heart had torn off.

Rollan walked, but his heart just beat harder. He felt jittery, his blood fast, his body anxious for action. He wanted to find someone he could blame for all this pain and hit him. Instead, he ran. He skirted the houses, running beside the fence, working his body hard.

He came upon Pia's house and slowed. Voices drifted from her open window. He slowed his breathing and then crept closer, stooping below the window.

"Say what you will to Pia, Shane, but don't be a fool and expect me to believe your lies!" Tarik was shouting. Shouting. In anger, no less. He never did that. The battle of Dinesh's temple must still be haunting Tarik too.

"Tarik, please," said Shane, calm even in the face of Tarik's rage. "Don't worry about this. You know only I can keep Pia and her town safe."

Rollan heard footsteps on the gravel walk and started away from the window. It was Pia, carrying a pitcher toward the well. Inside, Tarik and Shane continued to argue.

"Overhear anything interesting?" Pia asked, lowering the bucket into the water. She looked tired, her near-constant smile unable to hide the sadness.

"Pia, listen, I'm not a Greencloak, and I'm not a fan of meddling in others' affairs. I think people should mostly just mind their own business. But I've seen what Shane and his allies do. They have no mercy. They kill anyone who gets in their way."

"And what is their way?" Pia asked calmly, pouring water into the pitcher.

"Destruction," he said. "Domination. No place is safe. If Shane is already here, the army of Conquerors won't be far behind. There's no use hiding from them. Nowhere is safe, and nothing will remain the same. Zhong has fallen. They're all over Nilo and Eura. Please. Helping us isn't a choice between keeping your extended life and losing it. It's a choice between any life at all and total destruction."

Pia nodded. This didn't seem to surprise her, and Rollan suddenly wondered if she was old enough to remember the war with the first Devourer.

"You know how to help us find Suka," he said. "Please. Someone's going to find her, wake her, claim her talisman. If it's not us, it will be the Conquerors."

Pia pressed her lips together. She looked out over the town, as if seeing it for the last time. Something in her face made him think she was about to lie to him.

But the heightened sounds of Tarik and Shane came through the window, and Pia sighed.

"Excuse me, I should return to my *guests*," she said.

She started back to the house. Essix screeched, circling overhead, and in that moment Rollan noticed Pia's hand straying to her apron pocket, as if making sure something there lay hidden.

Rollan rushed after her, catching her just inside the small kitchen.

"What are you hiding?" he asked, indicating her apron pocket. "What do you have?"

She was still smiling, yet somehow it looked more like a frown. Her hand went into her pocket, and he could see the indecision on her face. "I was going to give this to one of you. And I think you and your friends have a better chance of finding Suka than the newcomers."

Truth. She meant what she said.

A squawk startled Rollan – Essix shouting a warning. He turned to see Wikerus flying past the open kitchen door and flapping over to Aidana, who was emerging through a small copse of trees.

"Rollan?" Aidana called out, just as Pia dropped something heavy into Rollan's inner cloak pocket before hurrying back into the main room.

Rollan was addled by the presence of his mother, and he

didn't think to examine Pia's face before she was already gone. He opened his pocket and peered in – a compass. Why would Pia give him a compass?

He shuffled back outside. The sharp light of morning sun sliced at his eyes, and he blinked rapidly.

"Rollan, are you all right?" Aidana asked, coming nearer. "You ran off."

Must be a family trait, he thought.

But now she was here – his mother – alive, real. That face from his dreams wasn't just the vain imagination of a pathetic, lonely orphan boy. And his heart ached where that chunk had torn free.

"I'm sorry," she said.

And he believed her. She was sorry. Everything she'd said had been true. She'd been sick, mad, trying to protect him. And now she'd found him again. So why did he hurt so much more now than when he'd believed her long dead?

"Stay with me," she said. "Please."

Words of affirmation rose in his throat. He choked them down, glancing at the house where Tarik's and Shane's voices lashed out the window.

"Shane is good," said Aidana. "I swear it. I've seen so much good that he does."

"I've seen . . . other things," said Rollan.

"He is passionate about protecting the world from the duplicitous Greencloaks. They hoard the secret of the Nectar; they subject us all to their secret plans."

He didn't want to argue with her, but the words came out, pleading. "We don't need the Greencloaks *or* the Conquerors."

She shook her head. "Zerif saved my life, Rollan. I won't

abandon his cause. Abandoning you was hard enough – I won't do that again, not to anyone I care about. Besides, with the Bile, we're saving hundreds more from the bonding sickness. The Reptile King is turning the tide of power all over Erdas! Come join us. Be a part of the new world."

She held out her hands, as if yearning for him. Essix wasn't there to disapprove. So Rollan stumbled forward and almost fell against her. Her arms wrapped around him, warm and wonderful. He didn't lift his own, just let himself be held. He felt her cheek lay against the top of his head, her heartbeat steady against his chin. Part of him felt safe and whole for the first time in his life. And another part ached beyond belief.

6

DANGEROUS TRAVEL

ROLLAN WOKE WITH HIS HEART POUNDING. HE'D BEEN dreaming of a raven, wings as wide as the night sky, coming at his eyes, talons first.

Rollan wiped at his face with his sleeve, trying to scrub the image away. His shirt smelled like his mother's embrace.

He covered his face with his hands and took deep breaths to keep from weeping. He felt as if someone had pressed a wedge to his heart and struck with a mallet, splitting him like firewood. All those years on the streets, he'd carefully hardened his heart, building calluses like the ones on his bare feet. He'd worked hard to mold himself into a tough, unbreakable street kid. It nearly brought a laugh to his throat. He was so tough and unbreakable, yet even the thought of his mother almost reduced him to tears.

She'd been sick to madness. There was comfort in knowing that she hadn't abandoned him out of indifference, at least. And where had the Greencloaks been with their precious Nectar and lofty promises when his mother had turned eleven? They'd abandoned her too.

The Bile cures bonding sickness! This realization struck him with a force that nearly knocked him back. Abeke had insisted that Shane meant well, and here was proof that the Conquerors were doing good. They'd cured his own mother.

His mother. He had a family again.

Rollan eased himself onto his hands and knees, and started to creep toward his boots and cloak. The soft grass cuttings hushed beneath him. His hand pressed through the grass and hit a nail on the stable floor. Rollan's breath hissed with pain and he fell.

There was Meilin, her sleeping face turned toward him. He hadn't seen her look so peaceful, so content, in a long time. Not since before the Devourer and his forces had attacked them, unprovoked, and killed Meilin's father. Her family was gone, taken by the Conquerors, and now here his family was back, given to him by the same people.

He looked toward the door, his muscles shaking with the effort it took to remain still. His mother was out there, waiting, hopeful. But if he went to her, she would take him to Zerif and those other murderers.

He felt his leg muscles tense, ready to run to her anyway, so instead, there in the dark, he made a quick decision.

"Meilin," he whispered, shaking her sleeping form. "Meilin, wake up."

She bolted upright, hands defaulting into fists.

"We need to go," he whispered. "Now."

Meilin woke Tarik and Maya while Rollan shook Conor and Abeke. All put on their boots without asking questions.

They passed near the house where Aidana and her companions were sleeping. The window gaped open. Rollan's muscles still shook, but he kept his gaze straight and did not look inside – not to see her face one more time, to make sure she was okay. It was almost worse, not looking. In his mind he saw her sleeping restlessly, waking at dawn, looking for him. Finding him gone. But he kept walking on without a backward glance, and his heart tore just a little more.

Essix appeared, settling on his shoulder. The weight grounded his feet.

Abeke and Uraza led the way, the leopard's eyes detecting the best path in the dark. The pair was completely silent. Rollan followed Abeke through a break in the fence and waited until Samis was out of sight before speaking.

"Thank you," he said.

The group moved in closer to Rollan as they walked.

"For what?" Conor asked, keeping the farthest back, as if uneasy about walking near him.

"Thanks for trusting me that it was time to go." Rollan pulled out the compass. "Pia gave this to me. I think it will lead us to Suka, and I didn't dare risk Shane and the others overhearing us talk about it. I thought it best to leave while they slept."

"Well done, Rollan," said Tarik.

Rollan didn't admit the other reason. Perhaps if he ran, suddenly and quickly, he'd have the strength to leave Aidana.

And perhaps someday when the war was over, she'd have the strength to leave Zerif. The idea of a family – his own family, his mother – was a greater draw than any talisman in the world.

Rollan fell in beside Conor as they walked.

"Hey, Conor," Rollan said quietly. "Hey, Briggan."

The wolf turned his head and looked at Rollan with those blue, unblinking eyes. Rollan sensed disapproval.

"Listen, I just wanted to apologize," said Rollan. "I didn't get it – what you did, giving up the Iron Boar to save your family. It seemed selfish to me at the time. And . . . well, I get it now. That it was the *opposite* of selfish."

"Thanks," Conor whispered. "But I know it was horrible of me –"

"It wasn't horrible of you," said Rollan. "Or at least not nearly as horrible as some of the other horrible things you've done before or since."

Conor stared, stunned. "What?"

"That stew! That meat-grass abomination you made for us in Zhong was way more horrible. And that sheep joke you tell to everyone new we meet. Horrible! And your stench! Good gravy, it's like the passed gas of the Devourer himself!"

Conor gave a half smile. "You like the sheep joke. I know you do. I've seen you laugh."

"Yeah, you got me," said Rollan. "But anyway, the Boar thing? It was an impossible situation. And I've been a jerk to you. Sorry."

Briggan trotted closer, letting his furry back rub beneath Rollan's hand, and they walked in silence for a few moments. Briggan was big. Not Great Beast big, but still, fanged-and-furry-canine-predator big. On the streets, dogs were bad news. They'd fight you over scraps – or worse, chase you, snarling and rabid, one bite certain death. Now here Rollan was walking beside a wolf, his hand resting in his gray fur.

Uraza led the way with Abeke, but Meilin kept Jhi in her passive state. Rollan supposed the panda wouldn't be able to keep their brisk pace, still Meilin rarely let her spirit animal out. Unlike Essix, who was *always* out.

Rollan could sense Essix off to his left somewhere, probably taking a rest in one of the trees, since she could fly faster than the group could walk. Rollan whistled three notes trailing up, their code for *Come here, please.*

He heard the response: one falcon screech trailing down – Essix's way of laughing at him.

He hadn't really expected her to come. But it would have been nice. The weight of the gyrfalcon on his shoulder might have distracted him from the stinging weight in his heart.

"Have you been wondering how Shane and Zerif and all those guys always show up wherever we are?" Conor asked suddenly.

"Um, yeah," said Rollan. "You think someone is feeding them information?" Rollan couldn't help glancing over at Abeke. She'd been awfully friendly with Shane.

"Not Abeke," Conor insisted.

"Then who?"

No way it was Meilin. Or Tarik. Conor was just too honest and straightforward to be a spy, and Shane and Zerif had always seemed to find them long before Maya had joined their group. Certainly it wasn't Rollan himself. There had to be some other explanation.

Tarik was leading the way, compass in hand.

"Normal compasses lead to the true north – the very top of the world," said Tarik. "This one appears to be leading us north-northwest. Perhaps it's tuned to Suka or her hiding place."

"It better be," Rollan muttered.

It was dawn when they reached the rocky northern coast of Eura. With a lightening of the sky came a salty breeze that whisked over Rollan's face, cold as a slap. At this point, only a narrow channel of the sea separated Eura from Arctica.

"There's a village on the shore across the water," Rollan said, shielding his eyes from the glare of the cold sun overhead.

"Where?" asked Conor, staring.

"Can't you see it?" Rollan pointed.

"I don't see any land at all," said Meilin. "Just the sea."

"Your vision is sharpening," said Tarik. "Interesting. Yes, my map says there is an Ardu village on the coast. The Ardu only live in Arctica, but for a price they will ferry people across the channel – usually Euran hunters looking for seals or walrus."

"Walrus," Rollan said with a snort. He was determined not to be gullible. There was no such thing as a huge-tusked sea elephant.

"We need a way to signal the Ardu village," said Tarik.

"I got this," said Maya. She held her hand out, and her

salamander, Tini, scampered out of her sleeve and onto her palm. She whispered something to him, or breathed on him or something, and then carefully balled her hand into a fist with the salamander inside. She raised her fist above her head and Rollan heard a crackling sound, like the first twigs of a campfire catching heat. The air around Maya curdled with a smokeless heat, strands swirling, gathering slowly around her hand. He felt himself hypnotized, staring blankly at her shimmering fist. He started back a step when she opened her hand suddenly and a ball of fire the size of a saddlebag popped in the air above their heads. It rose, flickered for a moment, and then faded.

"That good enough?" Maya asked.

"I think so," Tarik said, smiling.

Some time later, a petite, bearded man paddled over in a canoe. He wore a caribou-hide cap with long flaps over the ears that dangled almost to his shoulders. The canoe was built of hides stitched together and stretched across a frame of animal bones, almost as if the canoe were the carcass of some hollowed-out beast. It reeked of fish and blubber; it was clearly a fishing boat, but probably all the boats were fishing boats there. Rollan stepped in, wary of the way the boat moved with every small lap of water.

Space was tight, so Briggan and Uraza entered passive state on Conor's and Abeke's arms. Essix circled far above. Rollan smiled up. He felt a little grumpy with her for refusing to come, but if he could fly, he'd be up there too, finding a good breeze and letting it carry the weight away.

Tarik paid the man a gold coin. He dipped in his oar and paddled away from the Euran shore with surprising speed. Rollan looked back, half expecting to see his mother standing there in the mist. She wasn't.

"Does everyone else have room for their feet, or am I the only one resting on a bed of dead fish?" Abeke asked.

"I've just been throwing the more disgusting ones out as we go," Meilin said.

The Ardu oarsman paused. "Excuse me?"

"Oh," Meilin said, and Rollan saw an expression flicker across her face that he couldn't quite pin down. It looked like embarrassment, but Rollan didn't think Meilin had experienced that particular emotion, ever. In her entire life. She cleared her throat and wiped her hands on the sides of the canoe. "I'm sorry. That was probably your food. I swear they were just the mangled ones you wouldn't have wanted to eat."

The Ardu turned, examining the water behind them. "Not all creatures are so picky," he said.

Suddenly, the canoe lurched, as if struck by a large rock. But there were no rocks nearby – no shore, and no land. Only water and what might be in the water.

"Take this!" shouted the Ardu, giving Tarik the only other oar. "Strike it when it surfaces. Otherwise, paddle!"

Rollan and the others began to scan the water, moving about nervously. "Stay still," Tarik said. "You risk toppling the craft without the help of the beast."

"Beast?" Rollan asked. "What beast?"

"There are predators in the water, Rollan," said Tarik, "the same as on land."

A keening roar rose from the side of the craft and Tarik struck something in the water that sounded like the flank of a wet horse. Rollan grabbed a handful of fish from the bottom of the canoe. "Should I throw some out?" he yelled. "To distract it?"

"No!" shouted the oarsman and Tarik in unison.

What could they do? Uraza or Briggan couldn't fight a creature in the water. The talismans seemed useless here – the Granite Ram's leaping ability and Slate Elephant's power to enlarge a spirit animal offered no way to battle a sea creature. And how could they fight something they couldn't see?

There was another hard thump on the canoe. The Ardu kept paddling, faster and stronger than Rollan imagined someone that small and that old could manage.

Lumeo sat on Tarik's shoulder, and the man put his hands in the water.

"Tarik!" Conor shouted.

Rollan watched, eyes wide, waiting to see some great jawed creature bite off Tarik's hands. But instead the water around his wrists shuddered, as if a stone had been dropped, sending out ripples on still water. Again, the ripples and a pulsing Rollan could feel beneath the boat.

"Tarik?" Abeke asked.

"Lumeo lends me some minor abilities with water," said Tarik. "I'm thumping at the creature with a push of water, hopefully encouraging it to leave us alone."

Several tense moments clawed past and the oarsman's pace slowed.

"I can paddle," Rollan said, worried the man was too tired to outrun whatever sea monster was chasing them.

"I'm sure you can, boy," the man said. "But we wish to get to the shore, not splash about like a wounded seal."

Rollan frowned.

"I believe we have outrun the creature," Tarik said, and the Ardu grunted. "Or at least it lost interest."

"Maybe don't give the giant people-eating sea monsters any more treats," Maya said, voice quivering. "Okay, Meilin?"

The motion of the sea started to make Rollan so queasy he forgot to be scared. Or sad. Or mad at the undervaluing of his paddling skills. At last the rocky shoreline came nearer.

"Hmm. I'd thought Arctica was all ice," said Tarik.

"Oh, there's plenty of ice, don't worry about that," said the Ardu with a mischievous smile.

"Wait, you haven't ever been here before?" Rollan asked.

Tarik shook his head. "But I have longed to. I want to know Erdas in all her different forms of beauty."

Rollan clambered out of the animal-skin boat and into the Ardu village. Small huts made of mud-and-grass bricks faced the sea. An elderly woman with bright blue eyes and a face like a raisin came out to meet them. Tarik spoke with her for some time, asking advice about how to survive in the icy north of Arctica.

"None live on the ice but those Ardu who bear a mark," she said. "My son drank the Nectar and bonded with a snow hare. He left us to live in the ice lands with his uncle, who had bonded with an ermine. Only those who have bonded with northern beasts can bear the eternal snows."

"Have you visited their village?" Tarik asked.

The woman shook her head. "They come to visit us here. We wouldn't know where to find them."

It was good they had Pia's compass, Rollan thought.

"There is much more hospitable land in Eura," said Conor. "Why do you live here?"

"We love it here," she said. "Our Marked relatives know where to find us. The wind and waters know us. And some nights, we lie back and watch the sky dance."

Sky dance? Rollan wondered if the cold and loneliness were getting to the Ardu people's heads.

The Ardu were happy to sell them provisions for the journey, as well as cold-weather gear – hooded cloaks made from thick caribou fur, gloves extending nearly to the elbow, high boots with roughshod soles, the nails hammered only halfway through to better grip the ice.

So much leather and fur; Rollan was sweating immediately, drops rolling down his back. It tickled and itched, as if spiders crawled beneath his clothes, and he cursed the ridiculously heavy clothing. Give him cold over heat any day.

Within a few hours he'd changed his mind.

Dirt led to snow, which led to ice. Endless ice, more than an ocean's worth, it seemed to Rollan.

The ice was mostly flat, with subtle rises and crests, as if mimicking the waves of a gentle sea. A fine layer of snow lay over the ice, chased by flickers of wind. The sunlight was bright, reflecting off a white world so that there was nowhere to look that didn't hurt the eye. After several hours of walking, Rollan closed his eyes and tried walking blind.

Rollan squinted his eyes open to get his bearings and noticed spots of black on the ice in the distance. Then they moved. The black spots were a nose and eyes.

"Polar bear," Tarik whispered.

"Suka?" asked Meilin.

Tarik shook his head. "Far too small. But even a regular polar bear is the most fearsome predator on land. We would be wise to avoid it."

They took a longer route, attempting to stay away from the polar bear's hunting ground, and then continued on north. They walked a half hour in peace until a snowbank immediately to their left unexpectedly moved, proving it had not been a snowbank at all. The polar bear rose to its full height, and the team froze. This terrifying creature couldn't be a "regular" polar bear, could it?

"Suka?" Rollan squeaked.

The bear opened a mouth the size of Jhi's entire head and roared. Rollan noticed blood staining the fur around the bear's mouth, and he drew back in terror. The bear lunged and swatted with a long arm, the black claws of its paw just missing Rollan. He had already stumbled backward in fright, and now fell flat onto the ice.

But Briggan moved in fast, hunched low, warning the bear off with a growl-bark-bark, growl-bark-bark. Uraza was loose and crouched, a threat gurgling in her throat. Maya fumbled off her gloves, closed her eyes, and smacked the fist of her right hand into the palm of the left. Sparks exploded out from her body like someone dropping a heavy log on a dying fire. The sight was spectacular, but the sparks dissipated quickly, even before hitting the ground. The bear watched the sparks fade, and then swung one heavy paw at a nearby snowbank, icy snow cracking with a sound like broken bones. Snow showered over the team, and chunks of ice went flying.

A piece the size of his fist struck Rollan in the shoulder,

and he sprawled back to the ground. When he wiped the snow from his eyes, he saw the bear several meters off, lumbering away in no apparent hurry. The polar bear, it seemed, had no predator to fear among their group.

They all watched in silence as the bear disappeared into the white plain, its fur indistinguishable from the Arctican surroundings.

"That was my big move," Maya whispered. "And it didn't even flinch."

"That was a regular polar bear?" said Rollan. "It was . . . *huge*."

"Suka will be much, much larger," said Tarik.

With Briggan alert for polar bears, sniffing and stopping to look as they walked, Rollan soon fell into a drowsy complacency. Surely no other danger could accost them out here. After all, nothing was visible but flat ice for miles and miles.

The walk was beyond wearying. The scenery never changed – just whiteness, the glare of sunlight. Beneath all those layers, he was sweating, feeling sticky and itchy across his back and under his arms. But his uncovered face was glaringly cold, nose running and eyes streaming, teeth in a permanent state of chatter.

"Meilin, did any of your tutors in Zhong teach you how to keep from shivering? I could use a lesson."

There was a sound to his left like a huff of breath and a moan. Was she annoyed with him for just asking that? He turned, feeling surprisingly hurt, and saw no Meilin at all.

"Meilin?" he said.

No sign of her. Anywhere. Rollan's stomach plunged. He shouted for her, hurrying back toward where he'd last noticed her out of the corner of his eye. He tended to keep Meilin in the corner of his eye a lot lately.

Essix screeched, startling Rollan as she landed on his shoulder. Her talons pressed against the front of his shoulder, as if warning him back. With the contact, his vision became even sharper, his awareness of his surroundings increased. He detected now a subtle difference in the ice that lay before him. And beyond it, a hole.

Carefully walking around the different-looking ice, he moved toward the hole. Lying on his stomach, he peered down.

A crevasse about two feet wide and perhaps a hundred feet long had riven the solid ice. A thick layer of ice and snow had coated over it, camouflaging it with the nearly identical solid ground. The crevasse was so deep that sunlight couldn't reach the bottom. And Meilin was clinging to the rough edge of the crevasse's icy cliff, about ten feet down. She looked up at him, her face a mask of panic, her frown frozen. She seemed unable to speak, to move, to do anything but keep gripping the tiny ledges in the ice. One slip and she'd fall.

"Meilin!" Rollan shouted. "Help, she's fallen!"

Rollan almost called for the Slate Elephant. Wearing it would make Essix large enough to carry Meilin, but the crevasse was too narrow. Great Essix's wingspan would be too wide to fit.

But apparently Abeke had had the same idea, because Rollan heard rolling thunder beside him.

It was Uraza. Great Uraza. *Huge* Uraza. Clearly Abeke was wearing the Slate Elephant, making her spirit animal the size of a Great Beast. The deepest parts of Rollan wanted to scream and run from the enormous thing charging at him, but he just stared. Uraza was like a monster from a storybook, a giant terror that shouldn't exist. He watched as a tremendous paw landed next to him, each claw the size of a man's arm, cracking into the ice, anchoring the giant cat to the frozen plain.

Uraza's huge shoulder muscles rolled as she crouched and extended one long arm. She couldn't quite reach Meilin. She crouched even closer to the cliff, knocking bits of ice down the crevasse. She reached lower. Her paw just managed to extend to Meilin's shoulder. Meilin hesitated to let go of her precarious hold on the cliff to grab the paw. Rollan heard her short, panicked breaths.

"Let go, Meilin," he said. "She's got you. Let go. It's going to be okay."

Though he didn't feel like it'd be okay. Meilin was one inch from falling into a bottomless crevasse.

"Okay." Meilin breathed out. She let go, clawing at Uraza's paw, hanging on by gripping handfuls of fur.

Uraza pulled her up slightly, curled her paw, and then batted her into the air as if she were a toy ball. Meilin rose, flying out of the crevasse, emitting a strangled scream. Uraza caught her in her paws, setting her down on the ice.

"Are you okay?" Rollan asked. "Are you all right? Meilin?"

Meilin stood on her feet, straightening her spine.

"I feel . . . a great deal . . . like a mouse," she said, wobbling slightly.

"What happened?" Conor asked.

Meilin cleared her throat, as if trying to get her voice

to stop shaking. "It would seem that some ice is false ice. Covering deep holes."

Uraza began shivering, and the ground shuddered with the sheer magnitude of it. Abeke lifted the Slate Elephant so it was no longer in contact with her skin, and Uraza flickered back to big-kitty size. Then Abeke pulled up the sleeve of her coat, and the leopard became a mark on her skin. "Some of us are more accustomed to warmth," she said.

"My pack fell down," Meilin said. "And with it, a third of our food."

Everyone groaned. They'd been traveling light as it was. Tarik had them all unpack, divvying up the remaining food equally between all the packs.

"It was foolish of me to put all the food in only three packs," he said. "I'm sorry, team, but the days will be lean."

Rollan shouldered his new pack, full of food, a bedroll, and part of their tent. It was heavy, though he wished it were heavier with food. He got an uncomfortable feeling they were about to starve in this icy desert.

Tarik brought out his long, thin rope, knotting it through everyone's belt with several feet between.

"Better keep animals in passive form," he said. "We don't have enough rope to secure them to us . . . or food to spare to feed them."

"Sure, let me just . . ." Rollan pulled up his sleeve, whistling to Essix. She whistled back that dipping, laughing note. "Huh, Essix won't obey me. What a shocker."

"We don't even know how far we have to go," said Conor. "We could run out of food before reaching Suka!"

"Do you wish to return?" asked Tarik.

Conor considered, then shook his head. He pulled up his sleeve and Briggan disappeared.

Rollan sighed and looked up at Essix.

"Did you see that, girl?" Rollan said. "Come on now, you pretty birdie." He offered her his arm with his most charming smile on his face.

Essix landed on his shoulders and ruffled his hair with her beak, like an older sibling rubbing a fist against a younger brother's head. A gyrfalcon was native to northern climates anyway. And she could hunt for herself. Passive state offered her nothing that she wanted or needed.

Though for Rollan, the ache in his chest still as real as the ice beneath his feet, the chance to be unconscious for a while sounded like bliss.

They camped each night, all six huddled in their small tent. Rollan was too cold to sleep deeply, too aware of the others twitching in their sleep, breathing, snoring. Each morning he woke up feeling as if he'd been in an overnight street brawl.

All day they walked, the monotony of ice, snow, and hunger interspersed with the constant threat of death by falling.

Tarik had rationed the food to a hand's breadth of meat jerky, one dry travel biscuit, and one apple each day. Hungry and bored, they played a game as they walked called Best Meal Ever.

"Hot pepper sauce over antelope steak," Abeke said. "Heaps and heaps of black grapes. Honeyed bread braids with goat's milk pudding."

"Just bread," Rollan said, brushing snow off his coat. "A huge loaf of hot bread, crusty on the outside, soft as a sigh on the inside, smeared with melty butter and a great deal of raspberry preserves."

"Raw, fresh tuna, juiced with lemon and ginger, over a hot bed of sweet rice," said Meilin. "Mangoes so fresh they're creamy, and –"

Meilin dropped.

"Crevasse!" Rollan shouted. "Hurry! Crevasse, crevasse!"

He held tight to the end of his rope that secured him to Meilin and was scrambling for a foothold on the ice. The others were digging in too, Conor beside him, but the rope was slack. Meilin hadn't fallen down a crevasse.

Meilin stood up, dusting herself off.

"I just tripped," she said. "How embarrassing."

Rollan was the one who felt embarrassed at his overreaction. He felt his cheeks coloring. "So, um, Conor said you keep falling because you're so heavy, but I defended your honor," he said, helping brush snow and ice chunks off her hood and arms.

"I said no such thing!" Conor shouted, and Rollan gave him a grin.

"I am heavy," she said. "It's all these brains."

She tried to smile at Rollan, and the failure of it made his chest ache anew.

They began walking again. Rollan tried whistling quietly to Essix. If the falcon sat on his shoulder, he might be able to detect the crevasses before Meilin fell again. Essix swooped down, knocking his hood back with the air of her passing, but wouldn't land.

"Mutton pie," Conor was saying, "with egg-basted

flaky crust, stuffed full of tender mutton and potatoes and carrots and covered in thick, hot, salty gravy."

Rollan had never tried mutton. The Greencloaks served it sometimes at Greenhaven Castle, but with so many other choices, he'd turned away from meat that smelled exactly like what it was – old sheep. But just then, mutton sounded like the best idea since –

There was no ground. Rollan was falling.

"Crevasse!" he heard someone shout from above.

All he could see was a rush of blue ice and blackness under his feet. He felt his gut loosen and the muscles along his spine tighten and twitch, as if trying to flap wings he did not have. His entire body ached with an explosion of fear, bursting out from the center of his body. The world was quiet and as slow as an exhale, and he seemed to have a lifetime of a moment to realize that he was about to die. No ground beneath him. Nothing but darkness –

A hard yank on his middle. Though it'd felt like forever, he'd only fallen as far as the rope between him and Meilin. Through the crack he heard more shouts now. They sounded desperate.

He held on to the rope, scrambling with his feet on the ice wall, trying to find traction that did not come. His feet kept slipping.

A sound like thunder and then Great Uraza's paw lowered. Rollan reached up, the cat stretched down, but they were still a foot apart. The rope was too long.

Rollan clawed at the ice wall, hoping to find a handhold, but just drew back a chunk of ice.

"I can't get up!" he yelled. "I'm stuck! I'm stuck!"

"Take a deep breath," he heard Tarik call. "We'll pull and you'll push. We've got you."

Rollan breathed, shallow gasps leading to one slow, deep inhale. This was not a street crew, ready to abandon him at the first sign of trouble. They had him. They would not let him fall.

He felt a pull on his middle, and he angled his feet to climb the side of the crevasse and then haul himself back onto land. He brushed himself off with shaking hands. Essix landed on his shoulder.

"Hey, Essix, great job scouting for crevasses," he muttered.

Essix nuzzled her beak into his hood, bit onto a hair, and yanked it out.

"Ow," he said, but something about the gesture actually seemed sweet.

"That was horrifying," said Maya, staring aghast at the hole that had almost been Rollan's grave. She started to walk, pacing in a circle. "I mean, that was really, really horrifying. I hate heights. And you'd think here on the ground you'd be safe from heights but then those holes appear like monsters from beneath, ready to grab you and –"

"Maya!" With Essix on his shoulder, Rollan could see a slight difference in the ice. "Maya, stop!"

Maya froze. She looked at Rollan with wide eyes and then down by her feet. She stomped her foot near the crevasse and a chunk of ice tumbled away, and down, and down, into a hole that had not been there a moment ago. She watched the ice fall, through loose strands of red hair fallen out of her hood and whipping against her face in the wind.

Tarik put his arm around her shoulders and helped her slowly step back.

"Good catch, Rollan," Tarik said. "Let's keep moving."

"Pear-and-cream-cheese tarts," Maya said, her voice trembling. "And an entire roast chicken."

After a few more falls and near misses, the group was exhausted. But they had no choice but to keep trudging forward. Even with his sharpened vision, Rollan could see nothing but ice desert in every direction. He was too tired, too hungry, too hopeless to find any joke in the matter.

At least Essix must be getting fed. She left him to fly out, returning perhaps an hour later to sit on his shoulder.

But Rollan noticed he hadn't seen any blood on Essix's beak or talons, smelled no meat on her breath.

"Couldn't find anything out there?" Rollan asked softly.

Perhaps offended, Essix took flight.

"Wait," said Rollan. He sighed heavily and put his mitten in his pocket, pulling out his rationed piece of jerky for the day. His stomach instantly growled, as if furious with him. But Rollan held it aloft.

Essix swooped back, taking the jerky with her beak. She sat on his shoulder while eating it primly, holding the jerky in one talon.

Rollan's stomach protested again, and Essix stopped eating, as if she'd heard. There was one small shred of jerky left. She held it in her beak and tucked it into his mouth as if he were a baby bird. Rollan made a noise of surprise, but Essix chirped insistently, so he chewed.

Essix stayed on his shoulder for the rest of the day. With her near, Rollan led the way, able to detect the difference in the ice that hid the crevasses.

That night, the others were so exhausted they fell asleep at once. Though Rollan's body felt bruised and spent, his mind couldn't stop thinking.

Ma, he thought.

Had he done the right thing to run away?

The Bile cures bonding sickness, he thought. *My mother returned for me. Are the Conquerors really just "Bad Guys"?*

He knew he was doing good with the Greencloaks, but there was more to the story than they were telling him, and that made him nervous.

He slipped out of the tent to search for Essix, but looked up with a gasp.

At first he thought smoke filled the sky – only the smoke was green and tinged with purple. But the colors moved like a slow-flowing river, lower than the stars. Arctica was wild, wicked, and dangerous, but he understood a bit why the Ardu stayed. He leaned back, looking up as long as his legs would allow.

Rollan smiled. And the sky danced.

7

COMPASS

THEIR FIFTH DAY IN ARCTICA DAWNED WITH A STRANGE GREEN hue. Abeke stared through the flap of the tent at the unnatural shade of sky, trying to warm herself with it, convince herself she was okay. She didn't remember sleeping all night. It felt more like she'd been knocked over the head and thrown onto the ground and had just laid there, feeling woozy with cold.

She exhaled heavily and watched her breath crystallize in the air above her and then snow back down onto her face.

Full morning came; the sunlight turned bright gold, but the air felt no warmer. Still, Abeke told herself she was okay. At least a mountain range in the distance now gave them a destination to walk toward in the otherwise endlessly flat ice.

The imaginary-meal game continued.

"For the seventh course," Rollan was saying, "trout in a great deal of butter and stuffed with lemons and thyme, broiled till its skin is crispy."

Abeke was too cold to be hungry. She was shivering so hard, she tripped and fell three times in one hour.

The third time, Conor helped her back up.

"Are you okay?" he said.

Yes, she was okay. Hadn't she been telling herself that for days? Surely the others were as cold as she was. Just because she'd grown up in the hot plains of Nilo didn't mean she couldn't handle a few days on ice. But she couldn't get any of those words through her chattering jaw.

Conor frowned, removed his scarf, and started to wrap it around her neck. Abeke was surprised how much warmer she already felt. She tried to move her lips into a smile, though they felt like ice. Conor smiled back anyway. To Abeke, family had meant a father and a sister who lived in the same house, ate with her, scolded her, wished her different. Not until meeting Conor had she understood what it might be like to have a brother. Not till knowing him and the others had she begun to imagine a different kind of family.

She started to say "thank you" but surprised herself by saying instead, "I haven't been able to feel my feet for a long time."

"Sit down," Tarik ordered at once.

He pulled off her boot and sock, and Abeke sucked in her breath. While her skin was naturally deep brown, her toes had turned an unnatural black.

"Frostbite," said Tarik. He began to vigorously rub her feet, and his touch felt like hot daggers. Abeke pressed her lips together to keep from screaming.

"I know it hurts," Tarik said, "but we have to get blood flowing again or you could lose your toes. Or even more."

Conor sat beside Tarik, removed Abeke's other boot

and sock, and began rubbing. Now Abeke did cry out. The pain was one thing, but the humiliation was almost unbearable.

"I . . ." she began, leaning forward.

"Stop it," Conor said, almost as if he knew what she was thinking. "On a snowy night watch, Euran shepherds can get frostbite. I've done this before, so stop worrying and just let me help."

Abeke covered her face with her hands. In one way, a boy her own age was rubbing her foot and that made her want to dig a hole to crawl in and die. In another, her friend Conor was rubbing her foot, which was one of the kindest, most humble things anyone had ever done for her.

This is what family does, she thought.

Shane had said to her, so long ago now it seemed, that they must find family wherever they could.

She lowered her hands from her face.

"Thank you," she managed to say at last.

Her feeling restored, they all hobbled on, finally reaching the mountain range that had been on the horizon for two days. It wasn't until she stood at its base that Abeke really understood its height.

"I would never attempt to scale such a mountain if our compass did not point that way," said Tarik. "We don't have enough food stores to waste time looking for a way around."

Mountain was perhaps the wrong word, because Abeke could detect no rock in it. It seemed, rather, that long ago in a great act of violence something had erupted up from below, pushing a range of ice onto the surface. Huge shafts of deep blue ice jutted together, building up and rising so high that Abeke expected to see clouds at the peak.

They all sighed.

"Up?" said Meilin.

They began to climb.

Abeke instantly wished for Uraza. With the enhanced abilities the leopard's presence gave her, Abeke would have no trouble leaping from pinnacle to pinnacle. But it was too cold for the leopard, and there was no food for her.

They climbed for hours, and though they were so far above the tundra floor that looking down made Abeke feel dizzy, they didn't seem to be any closer to the peak. Staying roped together saved them again and again. Climbing on ice was just a bit slippery.

By evening Abeke felt so weak her forearms shook, even when she wasn't gripping ice. The others were flagging too.

"Camp!" Tarik called.

"What camp? How?" Rollan said. "We're on the side of an ice mountain!"

Tarik handed him what looked like a nail used to build a house for a giant. "Take the mallet from your pack," he said, "and hammer the tent's corner to the ice."

In a matter of minutes, their tent was hanging like a curtain off the side of the mountain, the six of them behind it.

"Cozy," said Rollan.

Abeke and Conor looked at him like he was insane.

"Joking," he muttered, as if out of energy to explain, lie, or continue the joke.

Tarik slid along the cliffside and pointed at a spot,

speaking to Maya. She placed her hands on the ice, a dim glow visible between her fingertips. With a crack-bubble-hiss, ice changed to water and water to steam, forming an indentation in the ice that to Abeke looked just big enough for a loaf of bread.

"No larger," Tarik said, and Maya made five more.

"What are these for?" Meilin asked.

"These are your beds for the night," Tarik said, cramming his own backside into one of the divots.

"Beds?" Rollan said. "I'd be lucky to be able to sit in something that small."

"Then, they are your chairs for the night," Tarik said. "Get some rest as best you can."

Abeke had just drifted asleep when a sound like tiny fists punching at the tent woke her. Peering out from under the flap, she looked up the mountainside to see thousands of chunks of ice rolling down.

"AVALAN–!" she started to yell, but Tarik reached over and grabbed her arm.

"Peace," he said. "It is only a hailstorm. Falling ice. Frozen rain."

Ice falling from the sky? Abeke leaned back into her hollow of ice, trying again to sleep. The side of a cliff wasn't her idea of cozy. She could feel the cold creeping back into her boots, working again at her toes.

They all rose at dawn, exhausted but tired of trying to sleep. The short night had worn them down, like wind beats at sandstone, and every step felt like trying to roll a boulder. Abeke was just about to say she wasn't sure she could make it, when Conor slipped.

He was roped between Maya and Rollan, but they were too groggy to catch him. The weight of three people pulled on Abeke's rope. She couldn't stop her slide. She scrambled for a hold, anything, her feet skimming over clear blue ice, and then came the sickening feeling of a fall.

She jerked to a stop, the rope digging into her waist with the force of her own weight. She gasped, trying to reclaim the breath yanked out of her, dangling above a cliff. She looked up. Tarik was braced against an ice boulder, straining to keep hold of the cord that secured them all together. And he was slipping. Abeke's unsupported weight was too much to hold on the slope of ice. Her weight was going to pull him after her, and with him, Meilin. Abeke pulled her knife from her belt sheath and cut the rope.

"No!" said Tarik.

But Abeke was already falling. She seemed to go a long way before suddenly thudding onto Rollan, who was perched on a ledge ten feet down. Her head hurt. Her knife was gone, knocked from her hand in the impact, and inches from her head, a sheer wall of ice dropped down two hundred feet. She didn't dare to so much as twitch, afraid she'd slide again.

Meilin and Tarik stood above, eyes wide and desperate.

"Rollan, use the Slate Elephant!" said Meilin.

Now that Meilin said it, Abeke wondered how she hadn't thought to suggest that before. The lack of food was making her thoughts sluggish, and great ideas seemed to be as far away as warmth.

"It's in my pack," said Rollan.

There was no hope in his words. Rollan was gripping the ice as firmly as she, inches from sliding down the cliff.

"Where's the Granite Ram?" said Abeke.

"I have it," said Tarik.

"Give it to Abeke!" said Rollan. "Get her to safety and hopefully Essix will cooperate and fly it back to someone else."

Tarik carefully dropped the Granite Ram to Abeke, mindful of the cliff. Abeke didn't take time to put the chain around her neck, slipping the talisman directly inside her coat. She winced at the cold touch of stone against her skin. Instantly she felt confidence in her limbs. Her eyes seemed to adjust, as if seeing the world not as a series of objects but spaces between perches.

Carefully she moved off Rollan. What had seemed a treacherous cliffside now felt comfortable. She offered Rollan her hand, helping him to his feet and to a slightly safer ledge.

She adjusted her feet, preparing for a jump, but the movement sent her sliding off the ledge. Facing a hundred-foot drop, Abeke slammed her foot down and leaped.

Her legs no longer shook from exhaustion. Her mind felt firm. She knew exactly what she was capable of, and she leaped up the mountainside, covering in minutes a distance that had taken them hours.

She paused briefly at the summit to see if the view revealed anything of their location and Suka's hiding place. But all she could see was more icy tundra.

Down she jumped, from ice outcropping to thin ledge to precarious ice boulder, with a speed and balance that filled her with awe.

She landed on the flat ground and looked up, searching for Essix.

She waited. No gyrfalcon. The Granite Ram was useless

if she was left alone on the safe side of the mountain.

Then, a slow, circling shape. Essix landed near her. She didn't look at Abeke, as if pretending she was just hanging out on an ice boulder for her own amusement. But when Abeke held out the Granite Ram, Essix grabbed the cord and flew back up the mountainside.

By the time the final party member had hopped down the mountain, they began to set up camp in earnest. Real camp, with an upright tent and flat spaces to sleep. Maya made a fire to warm them, though without fuel to burn she could not keep it up forever. Still, she melted ice in their cups and they all had a hearty drink of warm water before bed.

Abeke woke on the sixth morning firmly believing today the grueling journey would end. Suka was near. The compass seemed to indicate that. A couple of hours into their walk, the compass began to twitch softly in Tarik's hand. Two more hours after that, it was constantly vibrating.

So everyone's eyes were on the compass when, all of a sudden, it shook so hard the cover flipped open. Inside what should have been solid metal was a hollow compartment.

Tarik sucked in his breath. Abeke leaned closer as he pulled a scrap of paper out. He unfolded it, revealing two handwritten words: I'M SORRY.

8

THE ARDU

FOR SEVERAL MOMENTS, NO ONE SPOKE. CONOR COULDN'T read the words on the note, but he guessed it couldn't be good. The compass had broken open. They were stranded in the middle of an ice continent, and there was no sign of Suka.

"No," Meilin whispered. "No, that can't be right. That can't . . ."

Maya began to weep. Abeke could not seem to move. Rollan crouched down and punched at the ice.

"Rollan . . ." Tarik began.

"I didn't see it," said Rollan. "I was distracted by my – by that woman Aidana, and I didn't notice Pia enough. She must have been lying. If only I'd looked. I'm so sorry."

Abeke kept shaking her head. Meilin was turning slowly in circles as if looking for something in that wasteland of ice.

Conor saw nothing. A mountain range. A horizon. No city, nobody, no escape. Even if they walked south again, they'd run out of food long before returning to Eura. All this time wasted, Conquerors on the move. Perhaps that rascal Shane had already found Suka while the Greencloaks were wandering aimlessly through the most miserable landscape in Erdas.

Conor sat down as if pushed by a huge weight. He'd left home, abandoned his family, with the hope that his mission was noble. To die listlessly on a sea of ice wasn't noble. It was pathetic.

"Still longing to see Arctica, Tarik?" said Rollan. "Still eager to know Erdas in all her different forms of beauty?"

Tarik opened his mouth but then seemed to change his mind about what he would say. "Essix, perhaps, could help?" he said softly.

"Essix, can you see anything?" Rollan asked. "Please, fly high and use those sharp eyes."

When Essix complied, Conor felt worse. Even Essix must have realized how dire the situation was to do as Rollan asked without so much as a squawk.

With no better plan, they sat and waited, eating their meager rations for the day. Conor hoped his stale biscuit and bit of jerky would digest into energy and faith, but his sore stomach just absorbed them like desert soil absorbs a cup of water, none the better for it. Maya warmed the group with brief bursts of fire and tried to renew the meal game, but the thought of food was too depressing.

Tarik examined the compass, taking it apart piece by piece. "It was a real compass once, but Pia damaged it. It was leading us to nowhere."

"She never intended to help us," said Rollan.

"She would lead us to our deaths to protect her own artificially extended life," said Meilin, her voice as hard as ice.

Maya paced, and her breathing sounded strained, as if tightened against a sob.

Essix landed on Rollan's shoulder some time later. His shoulders slumped, making clear that Essix had seen nothing of use.

"At the top of the mountain, I didn't see signs of any city either," said Conor.

"What city?" said Rollan. "There aren't any cities in Arctica."

"No, I mean the Ice City. The song says that the Great Polar Bear sleeps in the Ice City."

"*If* the song is true," said Rollan.

"Songs are always true, in their way," said Conor.

Abeke nodded, and Conor felt encouraged to go on.

"I mean, the song is how we knew about Suka's connection to Samis, and it was right about that. She wasn't there, but she *had* been. Maybe there's other truth in the words."

Conor cleared his throat, gripped his crook, and began to sing. He didn't have a strong voice, but shepherds sang, so he had lots of practice, though he wasn't used to any audience besides a lot of disinterested sheep.

West of the sun, north of the drink
Over the backbone of ice
Deep in the rime without a blink
The polar bear sleeps in ice
In Samis home where she was known
They honor her with each breath
The bear breathes not one of her own

In the Ice City free from death
Hidden from the ruinous wind
They chisel city from snow –

"Wait, do you think *drink* could mean ocean?" said Meilin. "Because we're already north of the 'drink.'"

"That range of mountains could be the backbone of ice," said Abeke.

"So we're looking for an ice city," said Conor.

"Where?" said Rollan.

"Well, we're already north of the ice mountains," said Conor. "The other clue is –"

"West," said Tarik.

"Yes, and there's a line in the last verse about 'the waters lap the falling sun.' I bet Suka is nearer the western shore of Arctica."

"At the very least, the coast should provide us better hunting," said Tarik.

"*Any* hunting," Rollan muttered.

So they struck west. And walked. And walked. The sun full in their face at sunset and pressing against their backs at sunrise.

Conor tried not to count the days. Numbers made him feel hopeless. Numbers like two, as in two biscuits left, and zero, as in zero apples in his pack.

And the morning they ate the last rations of food, someone began to cry. Maybe, Conor wondered, he was the one crying. Or maybe they all were. He didn't have the strength to look up and see.

A screech startled him.

Essix was returning from one of her many scouting flights. But this time she was gripping something white in her talons. As she swooped down, Conor saw it was a snow fox. Hardly enough to feed six people, but the idea of even a little fresh meat made his stomach squeeze so tightly in anticipation he doubled over in pain.

But then, the fox wriggled. Essix hadn't killed it. She was hovering before Conor, batting her wings quickly against the incoming wind to hold her position.

"Take it," Rollan insisted. "Essix wants you to do something."

"Oh!" Conor grabbed the fox from Essix, holding it tight. Outside Samis, Briggan had turned the pack of wolves away from the caribou herd. Perhaps Essix knew that Briggan had some influence with other canines. "Rollan, pull up my sleeve."

When his forearm was exposed, Conor released Briggan. The wolf shook his body, as if drying his fur after a bath, and immediately began prancing about, more like a playful puppy than an adult wolf.

"Briggan! I know you're happy to be out, but can you talk to the fox? Find out if it knows where to find Suka? Or, find *anywhere* really. Someplace we can get food and shelter."

Briggan sniffed the fox, howled, and then paced a quick circle.

"I think he wants me to put the fox down," said Conor.

The moment Conor loosened his hold on the fox, it leaped onto the ground, stared at Briggan for a moment, and then took off to the west.

"Come on!" Conor said, running after it.

A destination fed his limbs better than a dry biscuit and bit of jerky.

The weary, half-starved humans couldn't keep running for long. They slowed, and Briggan followed the scent of the fox, who was now far out of sight. Though surely not as strong as Briggan's sense of smell, Conor's own had sharpened so that he thought he too could detect a slight musk on the ice.

Rollan was the first to see something on the horizon. As they drew nearer, Conor made out about a dozen low structures with rounded tops. They were built from the ice itself – blocks cut out, stacked, and sealed together with ice.

"The Ice City!" said Conor.

"If that's a city, then I'm an army," said Rollan.

Several dogs had shown themselves, barking madly at the travelers. People stood behind the dogs, ivory-tipped spears and bone knives in hand. Conor could see many other animals – snow foxes, Arctican gulls, seals, snow hares and snowy owls, ermines, a musk ox, and two tall, great-antlered caribou.

"An Ardu settlement," Tarik said. "I can't imagine they'll take kindly to strangers."

Briggan trotted forward and barked too. The dogs yipped, then quieted.

An Ardu man with a spear came forward. The thick fur of his hood nearly hid his face, but Conor could see his pale eyes widen.

"Briggan," the man said in awe.

He turned to the other people, speaking hurriedly.

"Time to impress," Rollan whispered.

Meilin sighed and released Jhi. Abeke let out Uraza, who stretched and yawned as if she'd just been napping. Essix settled onto Rollan's shoulder, playing along.

The Ardu leader laid down his spear on the ice. Behind him, the rest tossed down spears and bows, and Jhi and the other spirit animals returned to passive state.

"The Four Fallen!" said the man.

"Yes," said Tarik. "They have returned and bonded to these special children. We need your help –"

The man raised his hand for silence. "The help you need immediately is food and warmth."

Tarik nodded, grateful. With the promise of rest, Conor felt the strength drain out of him, leaving his arms and legs cold. Maya collapsed against the ice.

Tarik and Conor helped Maya up, and the Ardu led them inside one of the small, domed houses. There was room for all six to sit, leaning against the walls of ice. An Ardu woman set a wide, shallow pan of seal fat on the floor and lit it. A smoky fire burned happily, warming the space. Soon Conor was drinking a mug of warm broth. The heat made him sleepy. He finished the drink and lay down. He heard someone else begin to snore, just before sinking into sleep himself.

He must have slept the rest of the day, and all night too, because when Conor awoke, it was morning. He stretched, luxuriating in the unfamiliar sensation of a great sleep. Their nights on the fields of ice felt like a long nightmare, and any sleep managed had been thin and cold, a ghost of itself.

Tarik, Abeke, and Rollan were also awake, and Conor crawled outside to meet them. He stretched again, just to feel alive.

"Not to trouble you," Rollan was saying to the Ardu chief, "but breakfast?"

The chief laughed. "First, we hunt so we can feast the heroes."

The Ardu hunters were already outfitted with spears and harpoons and setting off.

"We should go too," Tarik whispered. "Hunting with the Ardu might help them trust us with any knowledge of Suka."

So the four of them followed the hunters. Conor did his best to appear energetic and competent, but he imagined the hunters to be silently laughing at the awkward children stumbling across the tundra.

He had hoped it would be a short journey, but they walked an hour or more, during which Briggan looked like the only one of them having fun. The wolf would run ahead, diving headlong into snowdrifts and pouncing on things in the distance that might have been mice, or might have been nothing. Suddenly Uraza pounced, rolling Briggan in the snow. She pressed her paws against his chest and bared her teeth in what Conor could swear was a smile. The wolf yipped and scrambled free, and the two animals began to roll around and play-bite each other like a couple of pups.

"Mine could take yours," Abeke whispered.

"No way. Dog beats cat," said Conor.

One of the hunters shouted as if announcing a find. As they caught up, Conor could see a hole in the ice, blue water filling it. Apparently in this part of Arctica, ice extended out over the ocean.

"A breath hole," Tarik said. "Seals, whales, and

walruses who live in the ocean beneath the ice need to come up for air."

Rollan snorted as if Tarik had told a joke. "Walruses . . ." he whispered.

The hunter motioned everyone down with his hand, pointing at Briggan specifically and putting a finger to his lips. He then lay down himself. From a distance, in his brown furs and on his side, he resembled a seal reclining on the ice. The teammates all did the same.

Conor lay with Briggan on one side, Abeke the other.

"More walking and cozying up on ice isn't the best for frozen toes," he said. "I'd hoped you'd get to stay at their village and stay warm."

"I'm okay," she said. "I'll just do my best to keep my feet from freezing. I don't want you to have to rub them again."

"Me either," he said, then felt stupid for saying it. It might have sounded to her like he hated the task, but he really just didn't want her to get frostbite again.

He cringed behind his fur collar and waited.

And waited.

And waited, while his nose itched and his feet grew colder. This was a waste of time. Briggan was getting fidgety and so was he. They needed to find Suka! They needed to be up and fighting and stopping the Devourer–

A splash. A slick, brown seal nosed up out of the water, flopping onto the ice. No one moved. Two more seals followed. Still no one moved. Had they fallen asleep?

And then, as if by some soundless command, the hunters jumped to their feet, spears in hand, spirit animals appearing. The seals darted back to the holes, but the hunters threw their spears. Three spears struck the three seals, the wide ends catching. The seals slipped back into the water, while the hunters clung to the ropes that were attached to their spears. Other Ardu rushed forward, hammering small metal stakes into the ice. The hunters holding the ropes pressed their boots against the stakes to keep from sliding on the ice and being pulled into the water hole.

Conor and the others were all on their feet, ready to help, but soon the thrashing on the other end of the ropes stopped. The hunters pulled the seals back onto the ice and exclaimed, clapping each other on the shoulders.

Despite his hunger, the violence of the hunting bothered him. He hid a shudder, glancing at Abeke. While he'd been tending sheep in Eura, she'd been hunting antelope in Nilo.

"I guess it's the only way they eat," said Conor. "No way to farm up here. Either they catch seals or starve."

Briggan padded around, sniffing the seals while the hunters lashed them with rope, in preparation for a long walk back.

Briggan stopped sniffing and stiffened, head cocked. Listening.

"What is it, Brig?" Conor asked. Then he heard something too. A low groan, like the sound of something very heavy slowly rolling across the roof of a house – if the house was a mountain and the *something* was the moon. He looked around. Abeke was watching the hunters at work, Rollan was calling to Essix. Tarik was looking at him questioningly. Clearly no one else heard.

"Hey, guys," Conor began, "I think you should move away from –"

The groan increased. Still no one seemed to hear. Briggan spooked away with a yip. Conor tried to determine where the sound was coming from.

The ice. Below. There.

"Abeke!" he yelled. He ran forward, grabbing her hand and pulling her away.

"Conor, what are you –"

Abeke was interrupted by a loud CRACK. The ice where she'd been standing was splitting. Everyone was running now, but the lengthening crack was faster, and in a moment, Tarik was gone.

Conor saw the Ardu drop to their bellies, so he did the same, Abeke and Rollan beside him. Essix flew over the hole in the ice, screeching. Nothing disturbed the bright blue water's surface.

"Tarik!" Rollan yelled, crawling forward. Conor followed him, thinking to hold Rollan's ankles while he plunged in for Tarik. But then their Greencloak mentor appeared, thrashing and gasping. Something was pushing him up from underneath.

Tarik clawed his way onto the ice. Rollan grabbed his hand and helped pull, and they both scooted away from the crack. Behind them, the helpful seal emerged, sitting upright on the ice.

"Don't kill that seal! Please!" Conor yelled.

One of the Ardu women let out a quick, rough laugh.

"Of course not," the hunter said. "She's my spirit animal."

Conor stared, his mouth gaping for a moment, but quickly collected himself, hurrying over to help Tarik. Still he couldn't help but wonder if that was an awkward relationship, given the woman's diet.

Tarik was lying on the ice, shivering, his lips blue.

"We should go at once," said the woman.

"But, Tarik . . ." Abeke started.

"He walks," said the chief. "In this cold, he must keep walking or he dies."

Tarik nodded. He walked.

All but Tarik took turns dragging the heavy seals back to the Ardu ice village, where others took over, skinning the seals, preparing the meat. The women helped Tarik out of his wet clothes and into pieces of their own dry clothing.

Other Ardu offered snow-packed chairs for the travelers. Some of the villagers brought out animal skin drums, and amid heavy drumming and loud singing, the feast began. Conor's stomach was rumbling, eager, until he saw the feast.

Apparently the Ardu ate their meat raw. A woman handed Conor a pink, wobbly blob with a glistening chunk of brown meat clinging to it. The pink parts were the fat, Conor quickly discovered.

The Ardu sucked up the pink fat first, making slurping noises and humming contentedly. They made the fat sound so delicious, Conor's mouth actually started to water.

He took a bite. It was not delicious. It tasted like cold, oily, chewy fat. But Conor considered that in frozen Arctica, the more fat on the body, the warmer and healthier they would be. He slurped up some of the fat, swallowing it while holding his breath. The brown meat was smooth like raw fish and very salty. Conor felt as if he were taking a bite of solid ocean.

The girls were offered bone cups filled with wiggly white stuff, as if it were a special honor. They ate it before learning that it was seal brains.

"It was creamy," said Maya.

Meilin just shook her head and looked a little green.

Tarik held a small horn cup with a spoonful of the white stuff. He began to bob his head back and forth and sing, "Seal brains, seal brains, take some pains for seal brains. Better for you than your grains. Creamy, steamy seal brains."

Rollan and Conor looked at each other, speechless. Tarik stopped singing, restoring his serious face.

"I didn't just imagine that, did I?" said Rollan. "Tarik, did you just sing a song about seal brains?"

Abeke nodded, her smile broad, showing her startlingly white teeth. "I want to hear another."

Tarik looked so serious, Conor was certain he would never admit he'd sung such a song, let alone reprise –

"Seal brains," Tarik sang, "seal brains, my love for them it never strains. Just avoid the stringy veins in your pile of seal – I can't do it," he said, putting down the horn cup. "I cannot convince myself to actually eat seal brains."

"Now, Tarik," said Rollan. "You're spoiling your hardened warrior reputation. Go gnaw on some raw bones, quick!"

Tarik betrayed a small smile. "When I was growing up, if our mother gave us something unpleasant to eat, my brothers and I would make up a song about it to convince ourselves it was delicious. It worked well with lima beans and kale, but no song in Erdas can convince me to snack on brains."

Abeke took up the cup Tarik had abandoned. "I don't mind it. In my village we ate every part of any animal we managed to hunt, just like the Ardu."

As she lifted the spoon to her mouth, her eyes flicked to Rollan. Conor saw him nod a little. Rollan and Abeke seemed to share the experience of having to appreciate every last morsel of food.

Growing up, life hadn't been a banquet for Conor either, but he'd never starved. Even in the direst of times, there'd always been mutton, acorn and bullrush bread, wild asparagus, and boiled clover and dandelion. But in Abeke's arid Okaihee, or in Rollan's cobbled Concorba, there would have been few wild plants to gather or sheep to slay. Conor realized, even in his poverty, he'd been lucky.

But did his family have mutton now? Last he'd heard from home, times were troubled. They'd lost some sheep and weren't likely to have one spare. He bit into a purple slice of liver and tried to appreciate it on behalf of his family.

The feast went on all evening. Slice after slice of meat and fat, bits of organ meat offered up on bone knives. Then the rest of the seals – chopped up and slowly cooked over pans of burning seal fat – were offered in small bowls. Lastly, the women passed around small, pink rolls, which earned satisfied cheers from the Ardu. Conor took a bite and realized it was more seal fat, mixed perhaps with flour and something sweet. Conor surprised himself by taking a second.

"Mm, seal-fat sweet cakes," said Rollan. "Just like Mama used to make."

Rollan winced at his own joke for some reason and turned away, suddenly despondent. Conor supposed thinking about a mother reminded him that he didn't have one of his own. Conor's own heart pinched, thinking of his mother and what she might be doing right now.

"We thank you for this magnificent feast," Tarik said, loudly enough to be heard over the drums.

"Especially the seal brains," Rollan whispered.

Tarik cleared his throat. "We're on an urgent mission for the safety of all of Erdas. We seek Suka–"

At once the drumming stopped. In the silence, Conor became aware of the sharp sound of wind chiseling away at the tundra.

"We do not talk of Suka," said the Ardu man. "You may sleep here tonight. In the morning, you should go."

The Ardu showed the group to their ice huts, their mouths shut as if there would be no more conversation. Conor crawled on his hands and knees to get through the narrow opening of the offered ice hut. Once inside, he was surprised how warm and quiet the room was. It wasn't tall enough to stand in, but he sat comfortably on the flat ground, atop a pile of caribou hides. The others joined him, all spirit animals in passive form in the tight space. Except Essix, of course.

"Essix saw another settlement like this one a ways in that direction, and a third that way," said Rollan, pointing at two corners of their hut.

"Yeah, Briggan seemed to smell people off that way too," said Conor. "It'd have to be a lot of people to smell that far off, I think." He didn't mention that *he* thought he'd smelled people when the wind came from that direction as well. Maybe his sense of smell was sharpening, but the others might think that a little creepy.

"Why are they separated like that?" asked Meilin. "Why not all settle together?"

"Maybe they don't get along," said Abeke.

"Or maybe they're posted here like guards – watching over something that's in the center," said Meilin.

"The Ice City maybe?" said Conor.

"Isn't this the Ice City?" Maya asked.

"I doubt it," said Tarik. "It's small and looks recently built. Hopefully in the morning, after the feasting, the Ardu will be content and disposed to tell us what they know of the legendary Ice City. But no one mention Suka again."

Conor and Rollan both yawned at the same time, and then laughed.

"Let's get some sleep," said Tarik.

9

ICE CITY

ABEKE DIDN'T SLEEP.

She could picture the Ardu village, and the location of the other two settlements Essix had spotted. The three settlements formed a triangle. Briggan had smelled a lot of people. And Abeke smelled something fishy.

The positions of the settlements reminded Abeke of how her villagers had hunted a hippopotamus once. The drought was high, and food was rare. Three groups of hunters surrounded a water hole where hippos came to drink. They moved in slowly till the hippo had nowhere to run.

The Ardu were hunters too, and they'd surrounded something they didn't want anyone else to know about. When Tarik had asked about Suka, the singing and drumming and smiles had stopped. Clearly, Suka was something they didn't want anyone to know about.

Abeke glanced at the sleeping forms in the hut. She didn't want to wake anyone. Besides, it would feel really great to be a hero for once, to run back to camp and let everyone know she'd found Suka!

She was still wearing her coat and gloves. She picked up her bow and quiver and crept out the door.

Once outside, she released Uraza.

"I know it's cold," Abeke whispered. "But I need your added stealth. Help me find Suka?"

Uraza shivered, whisking her tail back and forth several times. Abeke led her to a small pile of seal meat she'd saved in the snow. Uraza grabbed it with her sharp teeth, and in three quick movements swallowed it all. She licked Abeke, sniffed the air, and padded out of the village.

A light snow was falling over Arctica; flakes as tiny as pinpricks twirled out of the way of Abeke's breath. With Uraza active, her whole body felt tight, agile, light as snow. When her boot stepped on the thin, fresh layer on the ice, the snow made no sound.

Even if it had, the Ardu had seemed especially drowsy after all that feasting. She suspected they'd sleep well tonight.

As soon as the ice huts were behind them, Uraza and Abeke ran. Through the clouds, the moon offered a dim blue glow. Abeke kept her gaze sharp, but Uraza noticed something before she did. The leopard slowed to a loping gait. Abeke followed.

An ice hole – but not like the breath holes they'd found earlier. There was no water beneath the ice here. This hole seemed deep and empty. As she crouched beside it, Abeke could see what looked like stairs cut into the ice, going down.

Abeke held her breath to listen and realized someone had followed her. She could hear the occasional crack of ice behind her, the hush as the soft layer of snow atop the ice was pressed by a small boot. Uraza sniffed the air, but didn't seem bothered. Someone Abeke knew, then. But if it was one of the group, why follow her in secret? Why not simply catch up and ask what she was doing?

Abeke's stomach hardened as she realized the answer – it was someone who didn't trust her, who wanted to spy on her. Someone who suspected her of being the enemy.

Abeke wondered what to do. Hide, and then jump out? No, she didn't want any unpleasant confrontation. She just wanted to find Suka's talisman, so they could all get out of this freezing-cold nightmare. Uraza pressed against her leg, her shivering body a silent plea.

So Abeke stood and turned around, whispering into the dark, "Meilin, is that you?"

There was no response, but after a few moments Meilin came forward out of the blue darkness. Usually Meilin stood with chin high, eyes challenging. Now her face tilted down and she didn't meet Abeke's eyes. Abeke pretended not to notice her embarrassment.

"I'm glad you're here," she whispered. "I suspected something was down here – hopefully Suka. Shall we look together?"

Abeke started down the steps. She tensed, waiting for Meilin to confront her, accuse her. When Meilin just wordlessly followed behind, Abeke finally exhaled.

The stairs kept going down. Above was darkness. Below was darkness. But she followed Uraza, who seemed confident that there was a way forward, not just a drop into nothing. The heels of Abeke's boots couldn't find purchase. She stepped lightly on her toes, her thighs aching as her feet tried to grip the treacherous ice. And then with a slip and a swoosh she was horizontal, her feet flying out from beneath her. She hit the icy stairs and began to roll, striking down against one after another, darkness pulling her down, no sense of how long she would fall, no idea where she would land.

She slammed into a warm, furry body. She seized Uraza around her neck and heard the leopard's claws squeaking as she dug into the ice. But Abeke's fall stopped. She kept gripping Uraza's thick fur, steadying herself as she got back on her feet and still clung as they eased down the remainder of the stairs into a pale-lit corridor.

"Meilin," Abeke whispered up the dark stairs. "Be careful, I –"

Meilin came into view, sliding down the icy stairs on her backside. Her chin was up as if daring Abeke to mock her.

Abeke let the corner of her mouth rise a little. Meilin's smile twitched in response.

They tiptoed through a narrow ice tunnel. It opened up, and both Abeke and Meilin gasped.

A long and narrow fissure had once cracked the ice, creating a huge underground canyon so long Abeke couldn't see its end. A thin layer of ice created a roof over it, like the kind that had concealed the crevasses of the tundra. The moon bled pale light through it, lightly illuminating the space with blue and silver.

"The Ice City," Meilin whispered. "It's *underground*."

Abeke nodded. She didn't dare make a sound. Though she couldn't see anyone, Uraza was sniffing the air in the way she did when sensing people. A lot of people.

First Abeke noticed that it felt warmer down here, though perhaps that was just protection from the cold Arctican breezes. Second she realized how quiet it was. All that ice muffled noises. Her own heartbeat seemed loud compared to the stillness around her filling her ears, insistent as the Ardu drums. Only the occasional crinkling and cracking of ice stirred the air, as ice never seemed completely at rest.

She left the tunnel and entered the Ice City.

The rift was much larger than the crevasses Meilin and Rollan had fallen into on their journey. This rift had cut a long, deep section of solid ice in two. Carved into each side of the ice walls was a city. Abeke walked down the narrow sidewalk of one side of the rift. Like apartments in a city tenement, room after room had been cut into the cliff. There were no straight edges. Everything was in arches and curves. Doorways were draped with hides. Abeke peered through a thinner layer of clear ice that served as a window. The inside of the room looked like a small home, with a table and chairs carved from ice and a great chunk for an ice bed. It was empty. Many were empty, but in some homes, people slept on the beds, wrapped with caribou hides.

"How is it glowing?" Meilin whispered.

Abeke shrugged. It should be dark down below, but a twilight silver graced every surface. Somehow the builders must have known how to best carve the ice so that it soaked up and reflected the little moon- and starlight that trickled down.

Every piece of ice was carved – the ground bore the

carvings of fine cobblestones, the great icicles hanging down were etched with intricate patterns. The front walls of the homes bore faces of women and children, of great warriors and hunters, of Arctican animals. The walls were frozen tapestries, the blocks of ice magnificent sculptures. Hundreds of years of carving showed everywhere Abeke looked.

Ice bridges spanned the crevasse. Abeke and Meilin crossed over, the arched bridge creaking quietly beneath their boots. In the opposite side they found more houses and structures carved into the ice walls and frozen art in abundance. What's more, they found stairs leading down.

Deeper seemed safer, and surely that's where Suka would be. So they descended and discovered another story of the Ice City, more houses and structures and art. More stairs and yet another story, and another, so that it seemed there would be no end.

Deeper they descended. The air seemed warmer still, though Abeke wondered if she was imagining it. Then the ice ended. And instead of ice, the rest of the city was carved from rock. No ice tapestries here, no sculptures, just walkways and stairs cut out of dark brown stone. They were so deep, Abeke wondered if they were in the center of the world. She felt pressure swelling inside her ears.

Deeper into the rock city, the air was definitely warmer. Uraza panted happily. Abeke glanced at Meilin to see if she would release Jhi now that she wouldn't suffer from the cold. Meilin lifted one eyebrow, perhaps guessing her thoughts. Jhi remained a mark on Meilin's arm.

Abeke and Meilin took off their coats and gloves, carrying the huge bundles under their arms. Torches lit the darker space, oil-soaked fur on bones crackling with fire. Finally they reached the bottom. They found pools of water, warm air stirring above it, and Abeke imagined how heavenly it would feel to bathe in such water. Surely the inhabitants of the Ice City used this lower level to wash, to drink and cook and thaw out from the harsh Arctican climate. If she had bonded with a snow leopard instead of Uraza, she could imagine finding this place a paradise.

"Suka is supposed to be frozen in ice," Meilin whispered.

Abeke nodded agreement. They wouldn't find Suka down here. She pointed back up.

So they climbed stairs till Abeke's legs shook, and she wondered if before Uraza she would have had the strength to climb all night long. But even without whatever aid Jhi offered her, Meilin didn't slow. She'd always been tough, but since her father's death, Meilin seemed to be pure, quivering energy.

At the first ice story, they took to the walkways and continued forward, the long narrow rift extending for perhaps a mile. Uraza's ears pricked up and she stopped suddenly, Abeke and Meilin halting behind her. Abeke could hear it – people. A mutter, a rustle. A few sleeping people turning over in their sleep. But they'd passed hundreds of apartments. Every Ardu living in icy Arctica had a spirit animal. If Meilin and Abeke were discovered, if the city woke and attacked the intruders, Abeke didn't think they'd have a chance.

But the noise quieted, and Uraza continued on.

At last they reached the end of the rift and were faced with the facade of an enormous ice building.

"A palace," Meilin whispered.

"*The* Ice Palace," said Abeke.

The exterior of the palace was thick, the ice a deep greenish white, except for the windows, which were layered with thin, transparent glasslike ice. The structure rose many stories high, supported by thick ice pillars carved with twining, frosty vines, topped with a triangular roof in a brilliant pure white.

There was no door in the doorway. They entered.

A great hall greeted them, tiles carved in the floor, delicate pillars holding the roof, a grand staircase with a huge chandelier of ice hanging above it all. Abeke knew she would never have time to explore each room, examine all the carved artwork in the walls, the details in each pillar and frozen furniture. No time to explore, because they had already found what they'd sought.

In the center of the great hall waited the polar bear.

10

FROZEN

SUKA DID NOT MOVE. DID NOT BLINK. DID NOT ROAR. WITH held breath and pounding heart, it took Meilin several seconds to realize the bear was sealed inside a perfectly clear block of ice.

She walked around the huge block. It was the size of a barn. She focused on the ice itself, its marvelous clear color, how smooth its surface was, as if it'd been polished by water. Fear nudged her heart, and she admitted to herself that she was avoiding looking fully at the polar bear.

I am my father's daughter, she thought. *I do not fear.*

Though thick, the ice was as clear as glass. She steadied her breathing and examined one bear paw, the strands of white fur caught as if in a breeze, the five curved black claws, each longer than Meilin's entire hand. Meilin braced herself and looked up.

Suka had been upright when frozen, standing on her back legs, her front legs lifted, in welcome or defiance Meilin couldn't tell. She bent her neck back, trying to see Suka's head.

"Up here," Abeke whispered.

Abeke was standing at the top of the stairway. Meilin followed, counting the stairs as she climbed: thirty-five. On the landing of the second story, they stood right at eye level with Suka. She seemed to be staring at them, her black eyes open, though so still. Her mouth was slightly gaping, and Meilin could see her long, yellow teeth.

Meilin calculated that five people standing on each other's shoulders would be about the same height as Suka. Though not as wide. Or heavy. Or as clawed or toothy or deadly.

Was it wise to wake such a beast?

"Look," Abeke whispered, her voice full of awe.

Meilin saw. Tied with a cord to Suka's left paw was a blue crystal carved in the shape of a polar bear.

"Her talisman," Meilin whispered.

Perhaps they wouldn't have to wake Suka. If they could just break through the ice and reach the talisman . . .

"We need Maya," said Meilin.

Abeke glanced around, peeking in a few rooms. "There doesn't seem to be an exit through the Ice Palace."

"We'll have to go back the way we came, through the city," said Meilin.

Abeke nodded. "I can wait here, guard Suka, while you get the others."

Meilin's skin was already covered in goose bumps from the cold and the frightening thrill of encountering this Great Beast. But at Abeke's words, the hairs on her arms stood up even higher. She looked at Abeke, trying to gauge her expression, read her eyes for any thoughts of treachery.

"Maybe I should stay instead . . ." Meilin started.

Abeke sighed. "Meilin, I've tried everything I know. I left home, I left the Conquerors, I joined the Greencloaks. I've slept beside you and fought beside you. What else can I do to earn your trust?"

Meilin felt anger bubble inside her. The sight of Abeke's face, innocent eyes, half concealed by darkness, made her fists curl. Abeke whose family was safe and alive in Nilo. Abeke who had hugged Shane, Abeke who might be conspiring with the enemy. Someone had to be responsible for what happened to her father – someone who Meilin could strike, make bleed, make pay. But she didn't need Jhi here calming her thoughts and helping her focus her mind to realize that someone wasn't Abeke.

"You stand watch," said Meilin. "I'll go."

Meilin ran all the way back through the sleeping city and up the narrow stairway. She emerged into a stiff Arctican breeze, the noise startling after the near silence of the underground. Pulling her hood back up, she ran to the village, thinking how Abeke would be better at this. Stealthier. Less likely to arouse the Ardu.

Why had she wanted Meilin to do it?

Could Abeke have a way of melting or cutting through that ice?

Meilin stopped in the center of a snowy field and looked back. The camp was far closer now than the Ice City. She continued on, though her heartbeats stung and her mouth went dry with fear.

"Hurry," she whispered to Tarik, Conor, Maya, and Rollan. "Put on your gear. Quiet. We found Suka."

The four didn't ask a question. They just started putting on boots and coats. In moments they were off again into the snow.

Meilin glanced back. Tarik's otter, Lumeo, was in his active state, a small, pointed head peering out of the neck of Tarik's coat. Maya's salamander was no doubt keeping warm and out of sight as well. Briggan ran beside Conor, occasionally biting at the wind. Essix was nowhere to be seen.

And the entrance to the Ice City felt miles away. Meilin's heart beat harder.

Had she made a mistake? Doubt seared through her. Perhaps Abeke had tricked her, played on her emotions to get Meilin to leave her alone. When she returned, the Crystal Polar Bear would be gone. Abeke would be gone. Meilin would be less trustworthy than Conor, who gave a talisman over to the Conquerors. And she would be that much further from avenging her father.

Meilin ran in front, and when she began to descend down the hidden steps, she heard someone gasp in surprise.

The gasps continued when they emerged from the narrow tunnel into the city itself.

"The song," Conor whispered. "The city artists made. The carved city. This is it."

Meilin put her finger to her lips and pointed at the nearest window, indicating that they weren't alone. Rollan's eyes widened, and Tarik peered through briefly, but they all resisted slowing to marvel at the city, following Meilin as quickly as they dared. The ice walkways had been carefully scored with cobblestone shapes, which minimized slipping. But it was still ice underfoot, and the ravine just to the side of the walkway led so far down that only darkness stared back up.

They hurried on in quick, careful steps. What would happen if the city dwellers awoke and found them trespassing?

What would happen if Abeke – and the talisman – were gone?

More gasps behind her when Meilin led them to the Ice Palace and to the pedestal of Suka. Meilin's middle felt as frozen as the city as she walked around the other side. No hole in the ice. The Crystal Polar Bear still tied to Suka's frozen paw. Abeke stood on the stairs.

Abeke smiled at Meilin, and Meilin exhaled and smiled back.

"There," Abeke said, pointing to the left paw. "Maya, can you extract that?"

Conor and Rollan were just standing there, staring up at the huge beast, their mouths open. Meilin rolled her eyes, but suspected she'd worn a similar expression when she first laid eyes on the monstrosity.

Tarik was running his hands over the ice, walking around the block as if measuring.

"We could never hack through this, not without –"

"Waking the whole city," Abeke finished.

"Yes, I don't think the Ardu hospitality would survive if they discovered us trying to cut into Suka's icy prison," said Tarik.

The four teammates looked around, catching one another's eyes. Meilin felt that they were all thinking, as she was, of past cities, past communities like Samis, who just wanted to keep things as they were. But Erdas had already changed and nothing could stay as it always had been – not in Zhong, not in Trunswick, not even in the wilds of Amaya, not anywhere for long. The Devourer's reach was long. Meilin was sorry to trespass on the Ardu, but she knew – like Conor, Rollan, and Abeke seemed to know – that no one was safe unless the Devourer was stopped. She believed in their mission. Collect power. Protect the talismans. Prepare to fight.

"Here?" asked Maya, pointing to the Crystal Polar Bear.

Tarik nodded. "As much as I'd like to meet Suka, I am hesitant to expose any of you to a beast that size."

"Look at those claws," Rollan whispered. "They're as long as butter knives. Sharp butter knives. No, *meat* knives."

"If we can free the talisman without waking Suka –" Tarik began.

"Come look at her teeth!" Conor called from atop the stairs.

"Okay, everyone, here it goes," said Maya.

She'd climbed halfway up the stairs and removed her caribou-fur glove from her right hand. A fist-sized ball of light formed over her palm. As Meilin watched, the pale yellow light spun, shades of orange and red streaking and pulsing together. Maya took a deep breath and blew. A thin stream of fire shot out, burrowing into the solid ice. A rivulet streamed down, forming a pool on the icy floor. A narrow hole about two finger lengths deep was scored into the ice, pointing at the talisman.

"Well, about twenty more of those should do it!" Maya said brightly.

She held up her palm and started again.

While she worked, Conor and Rollan walked around the barn-sized block, gawking at Suka.

"I dare you to touch it," Rollan whispered.

"You first," Conor whispered back.

"I'll carry your pack for three days if you lick it."

Conor actually seemed to consider.

"Boys," Meilin muttered.

Scattered around the ground at the base of the huge block lay knitted clothes, intricately carved walrus tusks, necklaces of ivory beads. Gifts the Ardu had laid at Suka's feet.

Meilin walked along the upper story, searching for a possible exit up to the ground. The Ice Palace was full of rooms – ballrooms, drawing rooms, bedrooms – all hollowed out of the solid ice and full of carved furniture. She imagined that, long ago, Suka somehow flooded this area with water – perhaps carving a channel from the ocean – and then submerging herself, allowing herself to freeze deep underground.

Perhaps the Ardu found frozen Suka years later when exploring the great rift and began to carve out a palace around her, and beyond that, a city. Year after year, sculpting and carving, turning every inch into a work of art. How must it be to live near a thing so awesome and fearsome as this Great Beast?

Meilin found no stairway up to the tundra, but she was just about to explore a room full of statues – animals of Arctica carved in huge columns of ice – when she heard Tarik shout.

"Wait!"

Meilin started at the noise. Till now, everyone had been so quiet. She hurried back to the landing.

Maya was standing with a ball of flame over her palm. She shook her hand, the fire dissolving into the air, and looked at Tarik with frightened eyes.

"Wait," Tarik said, whispering now. "It's cracking."

Around the hole, tiny splinters had formed with each enlargement; thin white lines radiated out from the hole Maya had burned into the thick ice. But now Meilin noticed two larger cracks moving away from the hole. Slowly. But moving. Spreading. Reminding Meilin of the time she'd pressed her thumb alongside a crack in a windowpane and made it grow longer. Maya had stepped back, as if waiting for the cracks to stop. But they didn't.

They kept growing. As if something was pressing–from the inside.

Everyone was still, breaths held, watching. Meilin was on the second level. She was at just the right spot to look into Suka's eyes. So she saw the moment that Suka looked back.

Meilin gasped and took a step away.

"She's–" Meilin started.

"Don't–" Tarik said.

Maya dropped her hands and backed up the stairs. Only Rollan moved forward.

"Suka," he whispered.

The shudder came first. Then ice cracking, the sound as high and piercing as the shriek of a kestrel. Then the eruption. The entire ice block shattered, shards and chunks exploding out. Everyone ran, ducked, covered their heads with their hands.

The gigantic polar bear lifted her paws and roared.

11

SUKA

ROLLAN TRIED VERY HARD NOT TO SOIL HIS PANTS.

He knew Suka was large. But frozen in ice, she'd seemed tame somehow.

Awake, in motion, she was scarier than street thugs looking for a fight, than a Great Ram thrashing, than an army of Conquerors.

Suka seemed to be death itself.

There was no intelligence in her eyes, only the wildness of a predator trapped. She lurched, cracking the rest of the ice block into pieces.

She roared. The people in the Ice City woke. And they screamed.

"Suka, wait!" Rollan started.

Suka staggered again, slamming into a pillar. The Ice Palace began to come down.

"Get out!" Tarik yelled. "Everybody get to the surface!"

The Great Beast roared, lashing out with her monstrous paws. Pillars fell, the ceiling cracked, chunks of ice began falling. The smallest of them could crush Rollan into oblivion. They had to get out of the Ice Palace now—but he also knew if they tried to flee the way they'd come, Suka might follow, and tear apart the Ice City in the process. All those people would be crushed or fall down the rift. No, there had to be another exit.

Up. Through a hole Suka had smashed in the ceiling, Rollan saw stars. Fallen ice created a heap he might be able to climb to reach the hole in the ceiling. Tarik saw it too.

"Go up!" Tarik yelled.

A huge piece of pillar fell right toward Tarik. At the last moment, he ducked and twisted in a motion that seemed impossible to Rollan's eye, barely escaping the falling ice.

Meilin and Abeke had been on the landing and were already climbing the icy rubble toward the hole in the ceiling. Beside Uraza, Abeke leaped from block to block with astounding ease. Meilin must have had the Granite Ram, because she jumped in great arches, passing even Abeke. Once up and out of the underground palace, she stooped over the hole and dropped the Granite Ram down to Maya, who caught it and began to leap up too.

Conor was trapped, Suka between him and the way leading up and out. Rollan hoped Suka might recognize Briggan as a fellow Great Beast, but her eyes were all wild animal rage. She swiped at Conor, and he ducked and ran, as fast as Briggan, as fast as a windblown leaf. His head low, he barely made it beneath the striking paw and beyond, and began to run up the fallen ice.

Everyone was on their way out of the Ice Palace but Rollan. He'd been on the far side opposite Conor and was crawling over fallen ice, trying not to draw the bear's notice. Now there was no one left to notice but him.

Suka turned, sniffed, and growled.

"Essix!" Rollan yelled. "Essix, please!"

He did not know what help she could provide. He didn't even know where she was.

Suka's paw came down. And the ice floor around Rollan began to crack.

Tarik paused, halfway up the rubble, and pulled Dinesh's Slate Elephant from the pack around his neck. He lifted it high, as if he would throw it to Rollan, but Rollan could see he was too far away. His otter-enhanced abilities didn't include a perfect throwing arm.

One more strike from Suka would end everything for Rollan. Either she would hit him this time, crushing him to bits, or she'd completely crack the ice around him and send him tumbling down.

"Essix!" he called again.

A falcon screeched.

Essix swooped through the hole in the ceiling and down into the crumbling Ice Palace. She took the Slate Elephant from Tarik, seizing the gold chain in her talons. The gray stone elephant dangled as she flew, looking heavy beside her petite body. She screeched again, and Suka looked away from Rollan to the falcon, swatting at the air. Essix dove, deftly avoiding her strikes, and flew right over Rollan. She released the Slate Elephant, and he caught it.

The ground beneath him shuddered, and a crack

widened, claiming one of his legs. He tore open the neck of his coat and pushed the talisman in, making contact with his skin.

A flash and Essix was as large as a flying wolf, with a wingspan as long as several grown men are tall.

Her shriek was so loud now, it cracked ice. Suka put her paws to her ears and roared.

Essix swooped, and Rollan lifted his hands. The ice shuddered again. He started to fall, his stomach full of butterflies. But he only fell a moment before he lifted again. Essix had snatched his coat at the wrists with her talons and pulled him up, her huge wings thrashing.

Suka swatted, just nicking one of Essix's wings. She dipped to one side but caught the air again and rose, barely fitting through the hole in the ceiling. They flew up into the startlingly cold air, all wind and snow, the hint of dawn bleeding yellow into the blue night.

"Yes! Thank you, Essix!" Rollan yelled.

Essix shrieked.

"Ow – but not so loud."

He was out of that underground nightmare, but he wasn't safe. None of them were. From below, more growls and crashes. Suka was tearing the palace apart. Cracks in the ice grew larger as the ground began to cave in. Tarik, Maya, and Conor had been standing nearest the hole, and now they ran away from it even as its cracks grew larger, seemingly reaching out for them. The Arctican tundra lay flat around them for miles, nowhere to hide. Suka would fight her way out of the collapsing palace. She would be free to pursue them and would be faster than any could run.

"Rollan, give me or Conor the elephant," Abeke shouted from the other side of the hole. "Only Uraza or Briggan have a hope of fighting her."

"Are you kidding me?" Rollan shouted back from the air. "No one has a hope of fighting her!"

Just then Suka rose up from the collapsing ground. At first only her upper body, but with one push and leap, the huge creature was free, galloping on four paws up the ice, straight toward Rollan.

Essix lifted again, and Suka rose on her back legs, reaching, swiping the air. Higher Essix flew, but Rollan wondered if it would be high enough. Suka's arm seemed to reach as far as the moon, her claws inches away from his dangling feet.

Essix's huge wings kept beating, and she and Rollan rose higher still, leaving Suka to land back on the ice. She swung her head around.

"Find Meilin!" Rollan called to Essix. "We need Jhi. A big Jhi, a Jhi Suka can't ignore."

Rollan couldn't see Meilin anywhere, but Abeke must have had the Granite Ram now. She was leaping in a huge arc over a crack, much farther than she'd ever be capable of, even with Uraza enhancing her powers.

Rollan's arms ached as he dangled from Essix by his wrists. And then suddenly, he was falling. Essix had let go. He started to scream –

Essix's talons seized him again, this time by the coat on his shoulders. She'd only let go to readjust. The position was far more comfortable.

"Thanks, Essix," Rollan said, his voice shivery with nerves. "Glad you still want me to hang around."

Suka was roaring. She lifted a paw to swat Maya. Maya tore her glove off her hand, produced a ball of fire, and blew. A wall of thin fire rushed out from Maya, blocking Suka. The polar bear reared back, her paw flung over her eyes. The fire dissipated quickly in the freezing air. There was nothing to burn, no wood or grasses to set aflame and create a barricade to hide behind. Suka readjusted to attack again. Maya responded with another wall of fire. But this time, Suka raked the ground with her claws, sending boulders of ice crashing through the fire. One struck Maya's leg. She screamed in pain and fell. Tarik picked her up and ran away from the polar bear.

Suka blinked and reared her head, looking for a new target. Conor was alone, running from the lengthening cracks in the ground. Suka moved toward him.

"Abeke!" Rollan yelled. "Jump to Conor! Get him out of there!"

Abeke crouched to jump but paused. The hole between her and Conor was even greater now. She couldn't get to him in time.

"Drop me, Essix," Rollan said, hoping to free Essix to go save Conor.

Essix started downward, but Conor was already sliding toward the hole, and Suka was getting closer. Essix kept hold of Rollan, surely realizing, as Rollan did, that she couldn't reach Conor in time.

Abeke took out an arrow, tied the talisman to it, and aimed high, perhaps adjusting for the extra weight. She shot the arrow.

The arrow struck the ice beside Conor's head. He broke

it off, grabbing the talisman just as the ground fell beneath him. Conor jumped.

His first leap carried him halfway across the crumbling crevasse, but not far enough. A huge chunk of ice fell below him. He slammed his foot down, pushing against the falling ice for a little more lift, and he leaped again, his arms circling as the ice cliff came closer. He almost made it, one hand reaching out to grab the edge. Abeke was there, grabbing his wrist and pulling him up.

Suka crouched on three of her paws, her fourth held to her chest, protecting the talisman. She began to run around the huge hole toward Abeke and Conor.

Abeke let arrows fly. The bear swatted them out of the air. A few stuck in her thick coat, not even reaching the skin. She shook, the arrows falling with delicate tinks onto the ice. Suka roared and slammed her paws down. Another crack formed in the ice, traveling at terrifying speed toward Abeke. Conor grabbed her hand and leaped just as the ice beneath their feet ripped apart, ice chunks tumbling down into a new rift.

"Suka, stop!" Rollan yelled. "Please! Essix, tell her to stop!"

He spotted dozens of shapes huddled at the far end of the huge rift. And then he looked closer and found that he could see even clearer.

"Thanks, Essix," he muttered.

Rollan could make out people emerging from the hidden stairs at the far end of the great rift, where Rollan had first followed Meilin into the underground city. They were huddled in blankets, having fled the Ice City too fast to dress. Some were barefoot. He also spotted lots of animals – snow foxes, owls, seagulls, caribou, seals – their spirit animals, all likely giving them a hardened ability to withstand the cold. They stood and watched, but they did not come to help. They would not fight Suka. Clearly they were brighter than Rollan's crew.

And running toward the Ardu, he spotted Meilin.

"Essix, there!" Rollan said, pointing.

The falcon flew Rollan with a swoop so low and so fast that Rollan's stomach seemed left far behind. His breath tingled with speed and icy air.

Essix passed before Meilin, dropping Rollan. He landed on the ice feetfirst, but tipped and rolled before regaining his feet.

"We need to gather the people from the Ice City," said Meilin. Rollan ran alongside her to keep up. "They have spirit animals, they can fight –"

"They won't fight Suka," said Rollan. "They built a palace for her. We need Jhi!"

"What?" Meilin stopped. "Jhi can't fight Suka."

"Of course not, no one could, not an entire army," said Rollan. "But maybe Jhi can communicate with her, calm her."

"Jhi's a *panda*!" Meilin yelled.

"A panda *bear*! Come on, you have to try!" Rollan yelled back.

He pulled the Slate Elephant from against his chest, and above him, circling Essix returned to her normal size with a muted screech.

Meilin's eyes were hot, and she seemed about to argue, but they could hear another Suka roar, and shouts from Abeke and Conor.

"Fine!" said Meilin.

She tore open the neck of her coat and slid the elephant against her skin, held in place by her many layers of clothing. Then she pushed up the sleeve of her coat. A flash of brightness, a leaping shape, and then Jhi stood before them. Except Jhi was no longer normal panda-sized. She was perhaps almost as large as the Great Beast had been in her prime. She was gigantic – maybe half the size of Suka.

Jhi looked at Meilin, huffed at a snowflake, and shivered. Suka roared, and Jhi slowly turned her head in that direction. She seemed to consider, then looked again at Meilin.

"Suka is awake and enraged," Meilin said softly. "She isn't talking, just trying to . . . to kill us. If there's anything you can do . . ."

Jhi looked toward Suka again. Two giant bears. One much larger, her clawed paws the size of boulders, her toothy maw like a gaping cave. The other bear smaller, slower, paws for climbing trees, teeth for gently nibbling bamboo, her shoulders shivering in the Arctican wind.

Jhi huffed air through her nose, then began ambling toward the commotion.

Meilin grabbed the arm of Rollan's coat. "She doesn't know how to fight. She's going to get killed. I don't want –" Her voice broke, and she took a shaky breath. "I don't want her to get killed. I don't want anyone else to die."

Rollan nodded. He reached out, took her gloved hand in his.

"We have to try," he whispered.

Meilin took another shaky breath, looked at him briefly, and her face softened.

"Okay," she said.

"Okay," he said. And he tried a small smile to show that it *would* be okay.

As one, they ran after Jhi, toward Suka and shouts and the impossible fight. They ran in lockstep, side by side the whole way, her hand in his.

12

POLAR BEAR ATTACK

MEILIN RAN. SHE WAS CONSCIOUS OF ROLLAN HOLDING HER hand, but the thick layers of their caribou-hide gloves made the touch feel safe, casual. A comfort. He wasn't trying to hold her, she wasn't trying to pull him. They were just doing the same thing at the same time, running toward danger together.

She was grateful for his closeness, because ahead of her, some eight hundred pounds of enlarged panda were padding toward the most frightening monster Meilin had ever beheld. Meilin wasn't used to this feeling, iciness dripping from her heart into her stomach, her legs weak and shaking. She wasn't used to intense, senseless fear.

My father's death weakened me, she thought vaguely.

Before her seemingly immortal father's end, death had never seemed truly real. Now it was. Now anyone might die. Meilin herself, Rollan, Tarik. Even Jhi. Jhi had died before – she might be killed again. A quiver in Meilin's heart warned her that she couldn't stand it.

Jhi was almost to Suka. The polar bear was standing on her back legs. She lifted her head to the whitening sky and roared. Meilin felt the roar inside her chest, Suka's confusion and pain vibrating with her own. Her arms felt heavy, as if she were back in Zhong holding her father's body, weighed down with heat and rage. In that moment, without Jhi and her friends to stop her, she would have done anything, hurt anybody.

"Jhi, be careful!" Meilin shouted. "Suka's not in her right mind!"

Suka slammed back down, her right front paw cracking the ice, her left pressed to her chest, again hiding the talisman. She opened her mouth, exposing teeth as long as Meilin's leg.

Jhi didn't stop, stepping around the larger chunks of ice comfortably, slowly and deliberately advancing. She was so large, her black markings were clear against the white background. Suka seemed mesmerized. She growled at the Great Panda. Jhi stood at Suka's flank and stretched her neck toward Suka as if to touch noses.

Suka leaned back, raising a paw. Meilin held her breath. With one swat, that clawed paw could end Jhi. But Jhi didn't duck, didn't retreat. She just looked calmly into the black eyes of certain death.

Jhi is brave, Meilin realized. *Fearless.*

Jhi stood on her hind legs too. Suka hesitated, clearly entranced by the sight of that huge panda – the movement of her dark limbs against a world of white, her silver eyes catching the dawning sun. She stretched her neck out from her hunched shoulders. Suka was breathing hard, almost as if she were afraid. But she let Jhi's nose touch hers.

Meilin could see the huffing of Suka's chest slow. Her paw lowered without striking. Jhi put one black paw against Suka's heart.

Suka dropped to all fours, Jhi beside her. They touched necks. Meilin wondered if through all that thick fur, their touch felt much like holding Rollan's gloved hand. She realized she was still holding his hand and dropped it, suddenly embarrassed.

But she didn't take her eyes from the bears. They were leaning into each other, Suka's eyes closed. Meilin had felt that peace Jhi radiated, at times intensely. Often she had rejected it, preferring to be angry. She held her breath, waiting for Suka to reject it too and attack again.

But when Suka opened her huge eyes, they'd lost their wildness. She looked at Jhi, at the Crystal Polar Bear still strapped to her left paw, then around at the various people – crouched, tense, ready to flee – all watching her.

"Jhi," Suka said. Her voice reminded Meilin of growls, of winds, of ice thousands of years old just starting to crack. It was a wild sound, deep enough to shake her bones, as lonely as an ice mountain in the middle of a tundra, as careful as a snowflake falling.

"Oh, Jhi," said Suka, "what has happened to Erdas?"

Jhi sat back on her hind legs and blinked. Suka nuzzled her neck, inhaling, then she sat back as well.

"You have returned," she said. "But you are not as you were."

Jhi turned her large head to look at Meilin. Sensing a request, Meilin pulled the Slate Elephant from beneath her coat, showing Suka. Jhi flickered in place and returned to her normal size, almost as if her gigantic proportions had just been a trick of the light.

"Ah, Dinesh," said Suka. "I see." She rubbed her eyes with one paw, as if seeing caused her pain.

Rollan approached. Meilin refused to be less courageous than he was and hurried up, walking beside him. She stopped next to Jhi, putting her hand into the fur of the panda's neck. She could feel her shivering, but sensed she wouldn't want to go into passive state yet.

"How long was I asleep?" Suka asked.

"Long enough for the Ardu to find you and carve an ice palace around you," Meilin said.

"And an entire ice city beyond that," Rollan added.

Suka looked to where the Ardu from the Ice City stood, far on the other side of the great rift. "The Ardu have always been my people. I hope I didn't hurt them. I . . . feel strange, after all that time asleep. My mind, it seems, took longer to wake up." She looked at Jhi. "Perhaps it never would have. But you were always the healer. When a healer joins a war, all should take notice. I should have taken notice."

Suka's eyes grew distant, as if she could see something miles away, beyond the view of anyone else. She breathed deeply. "Erdas is not what it was. I do not believe even you can heal her."

Jhi blinked.

Meilin looked for Tarik and Maya, but she couldn't see them. Perhaps Tarik had carried Maya too far away to see that Suka had been subdued.

"Suka, as you can see, the Four Fallen have returned," Meilin said.

Conor and Abeke had been edging closer, Briggan and Uraza beside them. Essix settled onto Rollan's shoulder.

Suka growled, and Meilin flinched, expecting another attack. But after a moment, she realized it was a laugh.

"Their falling was partly what drove me into the ice all those years ago," said Suka. "At my age, I should be wise, but I can only see my own folly."

"You hid yourself because you were afraid?" Meilin asked.

Suka's head turned to her, mouth slightly open, her long yellow teeth showing, and Meilin flinched. What in all Erdas could such a beast fear? Even calm, Suka was not safe.

Perhaps Rollan felt her shudder because he leaned closer to whisper, "Next time I'd like to meet a nice, cuddly Great Beast. Perhaps a giant bunny."

"I *was* afraid, in a way," Suka was saying. "The death of the Four reminded all of us that not even Great Beasts are completely immortal. I'd hoped by freezing myself, I might prolong my own life. But more, I hoped to keep –" She lifted her paw to look at the talisman and then pressed it back against her middle. "I'd hoped to keep my talisman out of evil hands."

She adjusted herself, and Jhi went closer, sitting beside her huge leg. She looked up, and Meilin noticed Suka's breath, white against the air, slowly exhaling. Jhi's presence was comforting her, encouraging her to go on.

"I should have fought beside you, Jhi," Suka said, her voice low and frightening. "And with you, Briggan, Uraza, Essix. What power I could have brought to you!" She slammed her paw on the ice, making cracks. "Regret drove me into the ice too. We Great Beasts have a stewardship over Erdas but a love of our own lives. The prideful belief that we'd always be greater than any man-driven rabble blinded us. Blinded *me*. You know, before I froze myself, Halawir the Eagle came to me, asking to *borrow* my talisman! I sent him on his way – minus a few tail feathers."

Suka laughed, the sound like an avalanche. But quickly her eyes saddened.

"But I had to ask myself, what did Halawir want with my talisman? I imagined what would happen if another Devourer arose and renewed the war, but this time holding all the talismans of power. I grew warier and warier. Better to remove myself from the world, preserve my life, and keep my talisman away from the Devourer and his Conquerors. But it was a useless act, wasn't it, Jhi?"

Jhi looked up at her and blinked. She nodded.

"You're asking for my talisman too, aren't you? You, like Halawir, want my power?"

Jhi looked at Meilin. She took a deep breath and spoke. "It isn't power we want, Suka. It's safety. For all of Erdas."

There was a pause, and for a moment nothing could be heard but Suka's slow breathing and the hushed groan of ice settling.

Rollan cleared his throat. "Dinesh gave us his Slate Elephant, as you saw. Arax would not give us the Granite Ram, but the Conquerors sought it too, and we managed to take it to keep it out of their hands. They have also claimed the Iron Boar."

Suka snorted in anger. Her exhale was strong enough to push Meilin's hood off her head.

"Please, Suka," said Meilin. "I don't think there's any point in hiding. Zhong has already fallen. We're all forced to take a side. I chose the Greencloaks and a fight for . . ." She looked at Jhi. "For peace." The word felt comical to Meilin, dramatic, a child's wish. Yet as she said it, she believed with a burning in her limbs that peace was the only thing worth fighting for.

"If the good guys don't get your talisman, the bad guys will," said Rollan.

Suka stared at him. Meilin noticed that Rollan flinched, but he straightened his shoulders and met the beast's gaze.

Suka exhaled again, this time ruffling the fur around Rollan's hood.

"Perhaps it's time for Erdas to enter a new age," said the polar bear. "Perhaps humans have become wise enough to be her stewards."

Suka lifted her paw to her teeth. With a snap, the cord broke. She caught the Crystal Polar Bear with her other paw and handed it to Rollan.

He lifted his gloved hands and reached over Suka's great claws to retrieve the talisman. Meilin noticed that his hands were shaking, but promised herself to never tease him about it.

"Thank you," Rollan said, his voice husky with emotion.

Suka rose up. "I will go. It's been ages since I ate."

Meilin heard Conor barely whisper, "I have an extra seal-fat sweet cake in my pocket."

"And I need to think," Suka said. "Times are changing. War is here. There will be a last stand. Do not be foolish, young ones. As you say, there is no hiding."

Suka bent over and gently touched noses again with

Jhi. Now Jhi's whole body was barely the size of the polar bear's head. The comparison reminded Meilin of a soft panda doll she'd had as a child. That had been a different life, a different Meilin. The memory of her old, safe bed with the plush panda startled Meilin with sudden sorrow.

Then without further warning, Suka ran, her four paws sending thunder through the ice. She headed north so quickly that in moments she was out of sight.

"Three talismans now," Rollan whispered, examining the Crystal Polar Bear.

"Well done," said Tarik.

Meilin turned. She hadn't realized Tarik had joined them. He stood behind, holding Maya in his arms. Her face was pained, her leg bound.

"Jhi?" Meilin asked.

Jhi lumbered over to Maya. Tarik laid her on the ground and carefully pulled up her pant leg. Maya flinched. The calf was already showing bruising, red and purple clouding her pale skin. And from the pain etched on Maya's face, Meilin guessed it was broken.

Jhi sniffed again and then licked her calf as a mother cat might clean her kitten. Maya tensed and bit her lip, straightening her leg.

"You should probably still splint it," said Meilin, "and be careful. I'm not sure Jhi's power can heal a broken bone, but her touch might help it heal on its own a little faster."

"What does it do?" Abeke asked, indicating the talisman in Rollan's hands.

"Let's find out," said Rollan. He considered, then offered it up to Meilin. She blinked, surprised.

"Go ahead," he said.

"But Suka gave it to you," Meilin said. "That means something."

"She gave it to *us*," Rollan said. "And you are a part of us."

Surely he meant all of them – the group. But when Rollan said "us," she heard "you and me." Rollan and Meilin. The thought startled her heart.

He tossed the talisman to her, and she caught it.

Sometimes back in Zhong, boys had offered Meilin flowers. In public, she'd been the general's daughter – pretty, wealthy, harmless. She'd taken the flowers with a bow, but secretly scorned those scrub-faced boys who only paid her attention because their parents encouraged them to make nice with the daughter of a powerful man.

And here was Rollan, the street orphan, Essix on his shoulder, in the middle of icy Arctica, offering her not a flower but a talisman of great power. And she was no longer the daughter of a powerful man. She was just Meilin.

She bowed to him as she would have to those bouquet boys. And she slipped the talisman inside her coat, placing the cold crystal against her skin.

At once she felt larger, stronger somehow. Her arms seemed to move differently. She lifted her hand, and Abeke fell over as if pushed by wind.

"Whoa," said Meilin. "Better stand back."

They backed away from her. Meilin moved farther from Maya, and then she punched the air.

The strength was thrilling. Her arms seemed to be longer, stronger, enlarged with huge boxing gloves made of wind. Her reach was long, the power behind her strike tremendous. She laughed.

"This is a little dangerous for close quarters," she said. "But with this talisman I think I could stand on the ground and knock a Conqueror right off his horse."

"Or steal a pie off a second-story windowsill," said Rollan. "I mean, not that I would do that sort of thing, now that I'm an upstanding hero and all."

She smiled and reached out, gently tapping Rollan on the chest from twelve feet away.

13

DEPARTURE

ROLLAN HOPPED AWAY FROM THE RUINS OF THE ICE PALACE with a smile on his face. He and his team had just faced certain death and come out victorious. He was . . . happy, he thought. It wasn't a feeling he was accustomed to, but it struck him more frequently since joining with Tarik on these insane Greencloak quests. Bright shafts of sunlight broke through morning clouds in the east. They shot through the holes and into the crevasse of the hidden city, making the walls of ice flash and sparkle like diamonds.

They'd found Suka. And not only had they survived, but so had the fragile Ice City.

"That's right," Rollan said to no one in particular, "I'm a verifiable hero."

He felt his smile fade as the group of Ardu men and women approached. About fifty Ardu with their animals had emerged from the city, but they were examining the great crumbling hole that had once been the majestic palace dedicated to Suka. The Great Polar Bear was gone, and all that remained of the palace was a jumble of sinking ice.

Rollan's eyes tracked the crowd, trying to find a friendly face, or even a younger face, amid the group of angry adults. His eyes settled on a girl who looked just a little older than him. He tried his most charming smile. She frowned even harder.

"Suka is gone," she said, in a voice so sad you'd have thought he'd killed her spirit animal.

And suddenly an enormous dog shambled forward to her side and let out some kind of demon bark. Rollan stifled a scream. It was the most horrifying dog he had ever seen. Bloated and brown, its snout was blunted and pocked with whiskers, two overlong canine teeth poking out from beneath them. Its ears had been shorn off, and it had flat, flipperlike paws that slapped the ice unpleasantly as it moved. Rollan shuddered.

The group of stern-faced Ardu stood silently till Tarik came forward.

"You will go now," said an Ardu woman with a seagull on her shoulder. She looked older than Pia – if Pia had never drunk the pond's water.

"We just –" Rollan started, but Tarik put a hand on his shoulder.

"We will go," Tarik said. "I am truly sorry for the damage. I'm relieved your city is still intact, but I understand you revered Suka and the magnificent palace that held her. If there had been any other way, if there's anything we could do –"

"You can go," the old woman said. "That is what you can do. Go. Now."

Tarik seemed on the verge of speaking again, but he hesitated, nodded, and began to walk, the rising sun on his left.

"Rollan, Meilin, Conor, Abeke, Maya," he called, sounding like a father gathering up his wayward children. "We go. Now."

As the mass of angry Ardu grew distant behind them, Rollan finally felt able to speak.

"Did you guys see that dog?" He hissed. "I almost peed my pants."

"He means the walrus," Meilin said. "One of the Ardu bonded with a walrus."

"Ah," said Tarik. "There you go, Rollan. You have seen a walrus."

"That was a walrus?" Rollan looked back. The walrus was in front of the Ardu, still watching. It howl-barked again. Rollan shivered.

"Creepy," he said. "I think I might not like walruses."

A few moments passed as they walked in silence, and Rollan felt the ever-increasing need to bring up a subject besides walruses and his fear of them.

"So what was with those guys, anyway?" he asked. "Those city Ardu? I thought they were going to cut loose with seal spears, the way they were looking at us."

"We freed Suka," Meilin said. "And destroyed the palace generations of their people had built."

"*We* didn't destroy it," Rollan said. "Suka did."

Meilin shrugged. "Part of who they are is gone, and it was our coming that made it happen."

Rollan saw the remembrance of Zhong burning in Meilin's eyes. He moved closer, till their shoulders touched.

"I guess," he said. "But I mean, what were they thinking a giant monster polar bear would do if it ever got out of that ice block? I would have put good money on 'smash, kill, and roar.'"

The wind shifted away from the brutally chilly west to the colder-than-imaginable north.

"Oh," Abeke gasped, and Uraza disappeared, becoming a mark on her arm. "I want to get out of here and never, ever return again."

"And how are we going to get supplies for our journey out of here?" Conor asked.

"I'm afraid the Ardu villagers will be less than welcoming," Tarik said as his otter flashed back into its dormant state.

"Because of the Ice Palace thing?" Rollan asked. "How could they know? I haven't seen any mail ponies, or mail walruses or whatever. I bet they don't know that we're the horrible palace destroyers of doom."

"Nonetheless," Tarik said, securing a rope around his waist. "We will be going directly west, to the coast. On our own." He handed a length of rope to Maya. "Secure this around yourself. Then Abeke, Meilin, Rollan, and Conor. Rollan and Essix have done a remarkable job warning us of crevasses, but I don't want to take any chances."

"Do you think Tarik wanted me in the back for a reason?" Conor whispered to Rollan once they were all tied up and walking. "I didn't do anything to offend him, did I?"

"It's probably just because you smell," Rollan said.

"Ha," Conor grumbled. "You smell at least as bad as I do."

"No, really," Rollan said. "I mean, like, your sense of smell is better. With your, I don't know, wolf-snout powers, you might be able to sense if we're being followed."

"Oh," said Conor, glancing behind them.

"But probably also because you stink," Rollan said.

After what felt like hours, Rollan could make out an Ardu village in the distance – a different one than they'd left, he thought. There were maybe a dozen people watching them. Rollan could see the glint of spears in their hands.

"Can they see us?" Rollan shouted over the wind to Tarik.

Tarik turned his head toward the distant village. "Probably," he called back. "Otherwise they wouldn't be holding spears."

"They suddenly don't like us?" Rollan asked. "They must think we're someone else."

"Or perhaps one of the Ice City's mail walruses got through," Meilin said.

One end of Rollan's rope was tied to Meilin. He tugged on it playfully, making her almost stumble. She gasped and tugged back. Hard.

Rollan flew forward, banging into Meilin. She grabbed him, trying to keep upright, and he grabbed her, trying to keep from falling. And for a moment they stood there, covered in leather and furs, and beneath it two people who were, essentially, embracing.

"Sorry," Rollan said.

But she didn't let go. He turned his face slightly, and the openings of their hoods brushed together. Her face was very close. Instinctively his mind whirled, searching for something teasing to say. But Abeke beat him to it.

"If you two are done playing kissy-face," she said, tugging on the rope.

Meilin and Rollan both pushed away from each other and began walking again.

Still, Rollan kept one hand on the rope that tied him to her.

About an hour beyond the last Ardu village, the wind began to grow so fierce that the snow it whipped up around them made it impossible to see more than a few feet. After Meilin crashed into Maya hard enough for both of them to collapse into a heap, Tarik called for camp.

14

MAYA

"IT IS AMAZING THAT I CAN FIND THIS COMFORTABLE," ABEKE said, sitting propped against her pack as the side of the tent near her flapped violently from the winds. "I actually feel warm. Is that odd?"

"Not so odd," Maya said, holding her hands over a hole she had hollowed out into their "floor." It was now warming the space with a small fire, seal fat burning in a pan as they'd learned from the Ardu. All six of them were crammed together, but the others were sleepy from the long day, already dozing against the pillows of their packs.

"That is incredible," Abeke said, leaning closer to the fire. She spoke softly, so their conversation wouldn't disturb the others. "All of our animals are fantastic, but what you do feels truly like magic."

Maya flushed. "Thank you, but to me, what you do, what all of you do, is magic."

"Summon our beasts? You do the same."

"Not that," Maya said, "though I think what you do

with that bow might qualify as magic. No, what I mean is how each of you can do this, all of this, and not be . . . be *afraid*."

Abeke closed her eyes. "I think none of us are without fear."

Maya nodded. "I'm sure that's true. But I guess I . . ." She took off her right glove and held her hand out to Abeke, palm down and low, as if worried someone else might wake up and see. Her hand was shaking.

"You're freezing," Abeke whispered. "Put your glove back on!"

Maya smiled. "Take my hand. Just hold it for a second."

Abeke took Maya's hand in hers, fully expecting to rub some warmth into it as Conor had done for her feet, but Maya's hand was as warm as if she was sitting on a beach in Nilo.

"I never really get too cold anymore, as long as Tini stays warm." At the mention of his name, the little salamander poked his pointed head up from under Maya's scarf and darted back under again.

Abeke looked down at Maya's hand in hers, shaking. She was reluctant to let it go. It was a comforting warmth to her own cold hands, but she also felt Maya needed something. Something she wasn't sure how to give.

"I'm not cold," Maya whispered, her voice hoarse. "I'm *scared*." She took her quaking hand back from Abeke and gripped both her hands together, as if trying to force them to be still. "What happened in the Ice Palace . . . the bear, the roaring, the walls broken, the ice shattering, the screaming . . ." She shut her eyes. "I almost died. We all almost died."

"But we didn't," Abeke said, smiling.

“We didn’t,” Maya said, returning Abeke’s smile with a sad one of her own. “But something in me – I don’t know . . .” She looked at her hand, still visibly quivering. “I don’t feel . . .” Her voice began to shake as hard as her hand. “I don’t feel right anymore. If anything . . . anything else happens . . .”

Maya shook her head, flashed an apologetic smile, and lay down, her face turned away.

Later, amid the sounds of sleep, as Abeke lay wondering how one could fix things that are broken on the inside, she heard the flap of the tent open and close. She sat up, wary of an intruder. All bedrolls were quietly occupied, except one. Meilin’s spot was empty, the overcoat she used as a blanket cast aside.

As Abeke began to shrug on her own topcoat, Rollan sat up, looked at her, and then at the empty bedroll. “Meilin?” he mouthed silently.

Abeke nodded, and Rollan held up a finger, as if to say “Wait.”

She did, but every second that passed she thought of Meilin out there in the snow, freezing without her coat. Finally she shook her head, twisted the toggles that would keep her outer coat on, and rose. Rollan’s finger became a hand, palm out, and then two hands. “Hold on,” he mouthed.

A few seconds later, the tarp parted, and Meilin quietly padded in. She lay down on her bedroll and began to snore.

Abeke raised her hands, palms up, and mouthed “What?!” to Rollan.

He raised his eyebrows, shrugged, and dropped back into his bed.

Abeke lay down, her coat still on, and crossed her arms over her chest. What was that? Did Meilin do that often? Often enough for Rollan to know about it, obviously, but what did it mean? Was Meilin broken too?

Abeke sighed. Obviously, her brain was not going to let her sleep much tonight.

She drifted, waking often at every noise, her mind trying to solve all the problems – Maya, Meilin, Shane, and the Greencloaks.

She must have slept for a time, because when she woke again, a faint glow bled through the tent flap. She wrapped her coat and bedroll around herself and went out, finding Conor sitting on his pack, Briggan beside him.

"It's peaceful, alone in the morning," Conor whispered, so as not to wake the others.

"I can leave you alone –" Abeke started.

"No, sit. You're not company."

"Um . . . thanks?" said Abeke.

"I meant," said Conor, "being with you is like being with family. You're someone I can relax with."

Abeke sat.

Conor laid his hand on Briggan, wriggling his fingers into his fur. Abeke released Uraza, and the leopard stretched and yawned, showing off her sharp teeth, and then curled up on Abeke's lap as if to get warm. She was much too large, spilling off of Abeke's legs. Abeke put her arms around Uraza's neck and lay her cheek on the top of her head. Uraza purred.

"It's so bleak and cold, no sheep for hundreds of miles," Conor whispered, "but the sun rises everywhere on Erdas. The sun is just as cheerfully yellow here as it is in Eura."

"But muted," said Abeke. "I miss the fierce strength of the Niloan sun."

She heard the rustle of movement within the tent.

"Was it a dream that woke you, Conor?" Tarik asked from behind.

"No," Conor said, fidgeting a little. "Well, yes, but I'm pretty sure it wasn't significant."

"Tell me," Tarik said.

"No, really," Conor said. "It was silly. It was, like, a shoe dream."

"I'm sorry?" Tarik said, confused.

"We were on the ice and we all had weird shoes," Conor said, as if embarrassed, but now committed to getting the story out. "Yours were furry and had tails that moved. Rollan didn't so much have shoes as tiny little wings on his ankles. Meilin had on boots that looked like dumplings, with really long green laces that seemed to trail behind us for miles."

"I see," Tarik said, the hint of a smile on his lips. "And the dumpling shoes shocked you to wakefulness."

"No, not that." Conor glanced at Abeke and back at his hands. "Abeke had, like, these fantastic slippers made from fire, which of course kept her feet warm, but also started to melt the ice. She started sinking down, and nobody noticed but me. I tried to run to her but my shoes, they . . ."

"Yes," Tarik prodded.

"They . . . they were walruses," Conor said. "Like, little foot-sized walruses with their tusks stuck in the ice. They wouldn't let me run. Abeke fell into the water under the ice, and then I woke up."

"If only it were true," she said. "I could use a good bath right now."

Conor smiled at her, but then he stared a little too long at her face. "Oh, you look terrible," he said.

Abeke rubbed her face. "Well, thank you. If nothing else, I can perhaps achieve perfect unpleasantness on this trip."

"What? No! Er . . . what I mean is, um, not that you . . ."

"You look *tired,*" Rollan interrupted, emerging from the tent. "I think that's what he means."

"Yes!" Conor said. "Are you okay? Did you not sleep?"

Tarik had walked to the opposite end of camp and was staring intently at the horizon.

"Rollan," he called. "Can you see the coast from here? It should be directly west of us."

"I had difficulty sleeping, yes," Abeke said. "Meilin's night walking had me worried and up thinking for hours."

"Wait, what?" Conor said. "Meilin was out walking at night again?"

"Yes," Abeke said. "Without a coat even."

"I can't see anything!" Rollan called back to Tarik, and then he turned to Abeke. "It's nothing. We've seen her do it before, and she doesn't like to be interrupted. Maybe it's a kind of meditation for her. Anyway, she always comes back."

"Is she sleepwalking?" said Conor. "The Greencloaks say sleepwalking is a normal part of bonding."

"Meilin is well and truly bonded by now," Abeke said.

A drowsy voice called from inside the tent. "Okay! I'm up! Stop calling my name!"

15

THE DOCKS

THE COAST HAD BEEN CLOSER THAN ROLLAN THOUGHT. TARIK assured them that it was only a few hours' march away, but Rollan had been convinced he was just saying that to raise their spirits. But now they walked with the afternoon sun angled to their right, the salty sea air thickening the wind. They didn't get too close to the water, afraid of thin ice, but Rollan's sharp eyes could see slate-blue sea and the sharp white cracks of waves.

The goal was to get to an Ardu settlement and get a ferry to carry them to Eura. They had stopped their march for the moment, and Tarik was investigating something on the ground. Bug droppings, maybe. It seemed to Rollan that they were stopping like this every few minutes.

"Are we lost, Tarik?" Rollan called, loud enough for everyone to hear. Essix, on his shoulder, fluttered her wings.

"No," Tarik said.

"Because it looks to me like we're lost," Rollan said.

"We are not lost," Tarik said.

They walked in silence for several minutes, which Rollan figured was a few minutes too long.

"Not that I don't enjoy a good walk around an entire continent of ice," Rollan said, "but is there a reason we didn't just go back to where we crossed to get here in the first place? As nasty as it was, at least we knew that route."

And suddenly Rollan was attacked. What felt to him like a giant centipede leaped onto the back of his leg, skittered up his back, and clamped onto his head. Rollan screamed. He was certain it was going to either eat his eyes or lay eggs in his brain, or both.

"Get it off!" he yelled, running in circles, too afraid to touch the thing with his own hands for fear of losing a finger to the thing's inevitable teeth.

And then, just as suddenly as it had appeared, the weight on his head was gone. He looked around and saw Lumeo scamper up to Tarik and crawl into his coat. Then Rollan noticed the laughing. Maya and Abeke were giggling, and Conor was bent over, laughing those deep belly guffaws. Color rushed to Rollan's face.

Meilin wasn't laughing, but she was smiling, which might normally have made him feel mocked, but for some reason it didn't. Her smile made him smile.

"Yeah, so I thought Lumeo was a giant, carnivorous centipede," Rollan said, laughing.

Only Tarik stayed exactly as he was. "We're taking a different route back to Eura, and Greenhaven," he said, answering Rollan's question as if he hadn't just scared the life out of him with an otter attack. "Because I want to avoid Shane and his people."

Rollan grunted.

"We have been stopping to look for seal holes," Tarik continued, "like the one over there. We are officially out of food. And what our animals have been able to scavenge will not be enough to sustain us."

Rollan had mixed feelings about this. True, he was hungry, and while seal would not have been his first choice of meal, he didn't mind it. It was really the stabbing and the skinning he didn't like. There were kids on the streets of Concorba who would skin and eat rats, but just watching one of the other kids skin a rat made him lose his appetite. It seemed simpler, less cruel, and slightly less gross to get his food from garbage heaps. Unfortunately, there were none of those in Arctica.

"Is the great survivor of an otter attack going to restore his honor by spearing us dinner?" Conor asked.

"Um," Rollan started, ready to bow out of the whole process, when he saw Meilin looking at him and for some reason abruptly changed his opinion. "Get me a spear," he said.

And then they waited. And waited. And waited. Realistically, Rollan thought, it had probably only been an hour from the short distance the sun had traveled, but lying motionless on the ice tended to make time pass very slowly.

After another ninety-seven hours – at least according to Rollan's reckoning – he thought he saw some movement. Rollan cocked his spear arm back. Something broke the surface of the water in the hole, and Tarik struck first, throwing his own spear at the mark, barely missing. There was a terrible cracking sound, and the ice buckled under Rollan's feet, pushed upward from below.

"Get back!" Conor shouted, and Rollan did, just in time to see a demon emerge from the ice.

"WALRUS!" Rollan screamed. He scrambled back, unable to do anything but point at the beast that had emerged from the ice. Tusks swung at Tarik, who darted to one side to avoid being hit, but his otter-enhanced speed did not match well with the ice underfoot, and his feet spun out from under him.

"WALRUS!" Rollan yelled again, still pointing, still scrambling backward, but afraid to tear his gaze away from the thing. Abeke and Meilin loosed their spears at the same time, but they missed as the walrus charged. Meilin dodged, sliding into a roll that put her next to Tarik, who was back on his feet. Abeke skittered backward from the galloping behemoth as its bulk plowed into her, knocking her flat on the ice. The walrus raised its tusks to strike, and Uraza flared into existence. The great cat let out such a roar that the walrus actually stopped.

Briggan and Uraza both leaped, but the walrus slipped back into the hole with a splash.

Rollan's backward scramble had stopped when he hit a snowdrift, and as the walrus disappeared, he realized he was still pointing at where it had been. Maya was beside him, pressed against the snowdrift too, knees pulled to her chest, eyes wide. Her eyes darted to his.

"Walrus," Rollan rasped, voice hoarse from shouting. She nodded, and he dropped his hand, sore from pointing so hard.

"Well," said Tarik, "we would make terrible Ardu hunters."

They started on again. Rollan was full of nervous energy, walking twice as fast as the others.

"That was not a seal," he said. "That was supposed to be a seal. That was a seal *hole*. But that wasn't a seal. That was NOT a seal!"

At the next seal hole, they waited again, and were at last rewarded with a seal – no tusks, no charging, no walrus rage.

Abeke's arrow struck the seal's neck. She knelt beside it and whispered, "I'm sorry to take your life, friend. My . . . my family here needs your meat to survive. I took a shot I knew was true and would give the least amount of pain. Thank you; in your death you have saved our lives."

Everyone was quiet for some time after that.

Tarik, Conor, and Meilin busied themselves with cleaning and stripping the seal of its meat, parceling out chunks to eat now and chunks to carry with them. Maya put some seal fat into their metal pan and set it afire, though it was too small to cook over. Maya could sear the meat with her power but could not maintain the flow of fire long enough to cook it properly. Most preferred to eat it raw, like the Ardu. Maya moved away, to stand alone and watch the sea, and Abeke went to her, putting an arm around her back.

They traveled in peace for two more days, living off seal meat and two mutilated somethings that Great Essix hunted. Gradually, rocky land emerged from the ice, and another Ardu village perched on its southern coast. Rollan didn't care about the boat, didn't care about crossing, he just wanted to trade them whatever property he had for a good chicken-and-potato stew, though a nice corn hash with sweet peppers wouldn't go amiss.

But the village didn't have any chicken stew. They had seal stew, and seal brains, and some kind of crustless pie with meat that was probably pieces of whatever animal it was that Essix had brought them. So when Tarik suggested they just take the boat and be done, Rollan didn't object.

This boat was larger than their last ferry, flat and wider, low to the water and not full of quite so many dead fish. As the boat approached the coast of Northern Eura, Rollan began to discern the outlines of small buildings and familiar shapes. He sighed, relieved. These looked like the proper buildings of his upbringing, the kind that people who eat chicken stew might build.

They clambered onto the docks and Tarik pressed something into the hand of the boat's captain, which seemed to make him happy. The man bent his head and whispered something to Tarik, who nodded, and walked over to the group.

"The captain has told me that something is wrong," Tarik said.

"Like it's warmer than frozen here, and it doesn't smell of dead seal?" Rollan asked.

"Like the dockworkers are missing," Tarik said. "The captain said there are always people from the village here when boats arrive, to help unload cargo and offer goods and services." He looked to the captain, who remained on his boat. He appeared to be waiting for something.

"What does that mean?" Meilin asked.

"It might mean nothing," Tarik said. "It might be a holiday for them."

The group visibly relaxed.

"Or it might mean the enemy is here," he said, and Rollan heard Maya moan.

"Why is the captain just waiting there?" Conor asked.

"We need to decide if we're staying," Tarik said. "Or if we're worried enough to go back to Arctica with the ferry."

"Turn back?" Rollan asked. "To the ice and cold and walruses? No, thank you."

"That's one vote for stay," Tarik said. "Meilin?"

"I say stay," she said. "Turning back is not an option."

"Conor?"

"I actually think it might be smarter to go back," he said. "Not for *good*, mind you, just . . . I don't know, this." He gestured at the empty dock. "This all feels unsettling."

"Maya?"

"Go," she said. "Leave. I vote we go back."

"That's two stay, two go. Abeke?"

"I don't know," she said, turning to look at the sea, and Arctica beyond. "It's so cold back there." She stopped, scanning the faces of Maya and Conor. She sighed. "I am fine with either. Whatever you decide, Tarik."

"We stay, then," Tarik said, and nodded to the captain, who began unlashing his boat for departure.

"We will stay together," Tarik said, looking at all of them in turn. "If we cannot find transport in an hour, we begin to walk. Together."

The boat began paddling away, and Maya kept pace with it on the dock. When she ran out of walking room, she stood there and watched it go.

"I smell sheepskin," Conor said.

"What?" said Rollan. "You smell sheepskin? That's just weird."

"It is," said Tarik, looking to the village before them. "I haven't noticed any clothing made of Euran sheepskin this close to Arctica."

Rollan saw Essix circling ahead, and his eyes drifted down to the top of a dock-facing building. There were people there, on the roof. The sun was just starting to fall behind them, making it difficult to focus.

"Shane," Rollan said, squinting. "And those impostor kids. That blond frog girl, Tahlia, and Ana, the one with the lizard. I think maybe one other I don't recognize."

And his mother.

His entire life, an awareness of his lost mother had lain against his heart, like an arrowhead too deep to pull out. But he'd tried to forget her those long days on the ice. He'd tried.

Rollan took a few steps closer.

"There are a lot of people," Rollan said. "On all the rooftops."

"Archers," said Meilin.

"We're outnumbered at least five to one," said Rollan. He amazed himself by keeping his voice calm.

"I, um, I don't suppose they would just go away if we asked them nicely?" Maya asked. She glanced back, and Rollan looked too. The ferryboat was gone.

"Probably not," Conor said, his hands balling into fists.

"Maybe," Abeke said, and everyone turned to her like she had told a rude joke.

"Really," she continued. "Let me speak to Shane. He can be reasonable."

"I have my doubts," Tarik said, "but you're welcome to try."

"Don't go without Uraza free," Conor said.

Abeke shook her head. "Shane hasn't released his wolverine. I would seem antagonistic if I didn't keep Uraza in passive."

Abeke walked several steps forward and waved. Rollan imagined he could see Shane smile, but he wasn't sure what kind of a smile it was.

"This is a bad idea," Conor growled. "That guy is a weasel."

The figures in Shane's group disappeared off the roof, but the others remained.

"I think we should stay with Abeke," Conor said, moving. "In case Shane tries to pull something."

"We're close," Tarik said. "I don't want to appear threatening. I . . . I rather think a peaceful solution is our best option with the current odds. Let's give her a chance. If something happens, she's quick enough to get out of danger and give us a chance to engage."

Conor growled again.

"I think you might be turning into a wolf," Rollan said.

Conor stared as Shane hopped down from the building's roof, waving at Conor like they were old friends.

"I want to punch that guy in the face," he said.

Rollan nodded. "Some people do have faces like that. Though I've been told mine is one, and I disagree. I have never wanted to punch myself in the face."

Rollan felt himself rambling. He shut his mouth and looked down, aware of Aidana nearby, watching him.

He'd left in the night. He'd abandoned her in Samis and

run like a coward from an uncomfortable decision.

"I'm moving in," Conor said. Tarik raised an eyebrow.

"Just there," Conor said, pointing to where the dock planking hit dirt. "I want to be on dry land."

"Okay," Tarik said. "We all go, slowly. Just there, like Conor said. A respectful distance."

"Oh," Maya said, her eyes searching the water as if hoping for the ferry to return. No other boats were in sight. "Tarik? I'm just going to sit over here . . . at the end of the dock . . . and . . . and watch the sea, okay?"

Tarik nodded, watching Abeke speak with Shane. They were walking slowly, almost idly.

"He's leading Abeke to those crates," Conor said. "Like a herder, nudging his flock."

Rollan wasn't so sure. Conor was often jumping to conclusions, but they *were* getting farther away.

"They're coming back now," Tarik said. Shane and Abeke had turned. Abeke waved to get their attention.

"Good news!" Abeke yelled over to them. "They've agreed to a trade!"

A trade? What did Shane have that the Greencloaks wanted?

Tahlia was suddenly beside Tarik, her hideous flat frog lying on the palm of her hand. "You will give us the bear's talisman." She smiled coldly. "And we will return Uraza to you."

Rollan frowned. Shane was next to Abeke, smiling as they spoke. Did he know what these two were saying? His hand was holding Abeke's arm like a gentleman might hold a lady, but his hand was directly over the tattoo of Uraza.

Ana, her lizard scrambling around her ankles, spoke in a soft tone, so her voice would not carry to Abeke. "Shane is too much of a diplomat, so Zerif made sure we came along and enforced the plan. He was *especially* hurt by Abeke's betrayal. We will return Uraza, after we have cut her from the Niloan's flesh. Perhaps the Greencloaks can bind the wound and make the union fresh, if you are quick about it."

Tarik had paled. Rollan thought all of this talk about cutting Uraza away was rubbish, but Tarik seemed to be taking something about it seriously.

"Now," the girl said, holding out a sack. "The talisman, please."

No one moved. Shane looked over toward their group, still holding on to Abeke, his brow furrowed. Somewhere farther inland, a dog barked.

"Wait!" Shane yelled suddenly.

Without warning, Conor released Briggan. The wolf leaped directly from Conor's arm to on top of Tahlia. Her frog dropped to the ground with a splat. Ana's lizard hissed at the wolf, baring needlelike teeth. Like everyone else apparently, Rollan was so distracted by Briggan he didn't notice Conor run until he'd crossed the space and rammed his shoulder into Shane's middle, knocking him away from Abeke.

"Leave her alone!" Conor shouted.

Other Conquerors, several with spirit animals of their own, moved forward to attack, but suddenly Briggan was there. And Briggan was huge.

Conor was wearing the Slate Elephant.

The wolf was the size of an elephant, his cobalt-blue

eyes cold with rage, his canines exposed with each mad bark. The Conquerors lifted weapons, but Briggan swiped at the first wave with his paw, knocking them flat.

Tarik whirled, sweeping the feet out from underneath Ana and Tahlia with a low kick, spinning into a leap that landed him directly behind them and ready to strike. As he did so, Rollan saw a bear of a man stalk from the shadows. He took two deliberate steps toward Tarik, clamped his arm underneath Tarik's chin, and began to squeeze.

Rollan ran toward Tarik, unsure what he could possibly do against this beast of a man, now holding Tarik off the ground by his neck. As Rollan sprinted, an arrow flew past his head close enough for him to feel the fletching. He stumbled, stepping on something soft and wet, which sent him sprawling. Tahlia screamed. As he skidded to a rest on his rear, he saw it had been her frog, now sitting splat in the dirt. He couldn't tell if he had killed it or not. Tahlia looked at him with rage in her eyes and drew a throwing knife.

Rollan threw up his arms in an attempt to protect his face from flying steel, but nothing came. He scrambled to his feet and saw Meilin engaging both Tahlia and Ana with effortless grace. They struck, she spun. They kicked, she twisted. It looked like she was dancing. Rollan watched, almost forgetting it was a fight until Meilin planted a fist into the face of Ana, knocking her flat to the ground.

Everything was happening so fast. Fights breaking out. The roofs in motion. Scores of Conquerors teeming toward them. Rollan ran toward Meilin to help, though she didn't seem to need it. Her moves were so quick, Jhi must be in active state.

Then he saw the panda, sitting in the shadow of a stack of crates. Rollan heard the release of arrows. He didn't falter, running toward Meilin. She adjusted something under her coat, faced the oncoming arrows, and punched them out of the air.

The Crystal Polar Bear, Rollan realized.

Punch after punch, the arrows came at her and Jhi, but Meilin's invisibly extended arms swiped them out of the air, knocking them off course before they could strike her spirit animal.

"This way," a voice said.

Rollan whirled. Aidana gestured frantically.

"This will only get worse," she said. "Come with me."

"I can't," said Rollan. "My friends –"

"I need you to trust me now, Rollan," said Aidana. Panic lit her eyes, and she seemed as fierce and as beautiful as a bird of prey. "Now, Rollan!"

She disappeared around a large, square building. Rollan raced to the corner where his mother had gone, the noise of the battle prickling at his mind like a swarm of bees, no individual words distinguishable until he heard a new voice, a shriek, something that reminded him of the sound he had heard a cat make once when struck by a passing cart. But this sound had words in it.

"STOP IT! STOP IT! STOP IT!" the voice said.

Rollan whirled to look.

And then there was fire.

16

FIRE

Abeke didn't understand. Everything had been fine. Shane had promised he could get the Conquerors to leave in peace if they traded him the Crystal Polar Bear for the Iron Boar.

"It isn't safe for any one group to hold them all," Shane had said, "no matter how well intentioned. We just need to understand each talisman. But we won't steal the polar bear and leave you with none. I promise I won't let them."

Power sharing made a kind of sense, especially if it would allow her friends to go free. But then Briggan had pounced, and arrows began to fly.

When Conor plowed into Shane, Shane was still holding Abeke's arm, and the three of them spiraled into a heap onto the cobblestones below. Abeke felt like the end of a whip, riding a wave of movement that ended with her head smacking the ground.

She rolled to one side, stunned. Trying to stand, her

vision wavered, and she dropped to one knee, blinking several times. She could feel the irritation of blood dripping down her ear, but the sight before her drove any other thoughts out of her mind. Men and women and animals everywhere, thrashing, swarming, fighting. Fighting her friends.

Her eyes were drawn to four or five animals surrounding Jhi. Two wild dogs, a common house cat, a goat, and a stag were just staring at the panda. They had to be some of the Conquerors' spirit animals, but they weren't attacking.

A soldier barreled into Jhi, pushing her sideways. He raised a sword.

"Stop!" Abeke yelled, but the sounds of fury around her were too loud to be overcome. She saw one of the dogs bite the soldier's arm before Abeke was knocked to the ground.

A body had rolled into her, and she felt sweat or water or blood spatter her with the impact. She reached out, uncertain whether she was in danger, but wanting to help, no matter who it was.

It was Conor. He grabbed her hand.

"Are you okay? You're bleeding," he said, pointing to her right temple with a finger that looked like it had been bitten by a crocodile.

"You're bleeding too," she managed to say.

Between her and the buildings of the village – were those archers on top? – a figure stood, hand raised. The sun was behind him, washing out everything but a silhouette, yet Abeke knew it was Shane. His hand was splayed out, high, as if trying to hold back a sky filled with a dark swarm of birds. No, not birds. Arrows. Arrows arcing up, up, up to the sky, and now down. It seemed to Abeke like hundreds of shots had been taken at the sun, and having failed to reach their destination, changed targets. To her.

Instinct took over, and she seemed to no more think about calling Uraza out than she thought about making her own heart beat. Even as the leopard leaped forward, Abeke leaped too, her stride lengthened, her strength increased.

Abeke landed and rolled. The movement made her head spin, and she was certain that had she not been as hungry as she was, her last meal would have left her stomach. A dozen shafts plunged into the earth beside her. Much fewer than the hundreds she'd thought she'd seen. She wasn't thinking straight. She felt herself start to shake as her body seemed to realize before her mind that when she'd leaped away from the arrows, Conor had not. He lay hunched over, head bowed, three arrows lodged in his back.

He sat up suddenly and she gasped, stunned he was still alive.

"Abeke!" Conor yelled. "We've got to get to Meilin. Get *behind* Meilin!"

He stood, dropping his pack, and the arrows with it.

"Only one got through," he said. "And just barely. I'll be okay."

There was another shout from Shane, and Abeke saw he had two hands up this time, waving them desperately.

There were more arrows. More than a dozen. More than they could dodge. More than they could live through. She closed her eyes.

The heat of the sun on her face disappeared, and she opened her eyes to shadow, a huge shape blocking the sun. She heard the sound of dozens of arrows hitting a target different than intended, like an awkward chorus of rugs being beaten clean, and she found herself still alive and arrow free. The shape between her and the archers moved, and the light caught a rippling of gray fur. Briggan! Great Briggan, made huge by the Slate Elephant, was nearly the size of a real elephant.

His fur was so thick, the arrows didn't seem to have penetrated his skin. Conor jumped on the wolf's back and raised his shepherd's crook like some kind of shepherd king going to war.

"Get on!" he shouted.

"I'll run with Uraza," Abeke said.

Conor seemed about to argue, but a dozen soldiers were running at him. The wolf growled a sound like the end of the world, and for a moment, everything was quiet but for the whimpering of several animals that Abeke could not see. Then the Great Wolf leaped at the soldiers, and it all began again.

Briggan scattered the men, grabbing one between his powerful jaws. Abeke heard a sharp crack and the Great Wolf threw the body aside to snap at an approaching ox and its rider.

Abeke ducked behind some crates as more arrows flew. There seemed to be hundreds of Conquerors, and no one was listening to Shane. He'd stop them if he could, she knew, but the frenzy of battle swept away all thought and reason.

A great maned lion pounced. Abeke only noticed a blur of yellow before Uraza's answering yowl raised the hairs on her arms. While the two cats fought, Abeke nocked an arrow. The swirl of golden bodies made targeting the lion impossible. She glanced up and spotted more archers on the roof. She saw one turn, targeting Conor on the back of Briggan. Abeke aimed and shot. The archer fell from the roof.

Uraza bumped her knee. The lion was still. Abeke put a hand on her spirit animal's head.

"To Meilin," she said.

They began to run. In her periphery, she saw Conor duck behind Great Briggan as more arrows shot from the tops of buildings, striking the wolf. It seemed impossible that his thick coat could deflect them all. And even the largest beast could be slain with sufficient ammunition and strategy. They needed strategy. In this kind of wild fighting, the side with the most fighters always won. And that meant she and her friends were sure to lose. And die.

Abeke looked frantically for Tarik, and found him struggling in the grip of a man twice his size, his otter thrashing crazily, trying to escape the coils of a tremendous boa constrictor, aiming sharp bites at the snake's head.

She ran toward the Greencloak, staying low. She aimed her arrow, but afraid of hitting Tarik, she was only able to shoot his attacker in the knee.

She and Uraza started for Meilin again, but were struck by a wave of force, a flat wall of wind that shoved her heavily off her feet, through the air several feet, and onto the ground yards from Meilin, who shouted something at her. The Zhongian was standing over the bodies of Zerif's two impostor girls, slapping wildly at the air like an old madwoman, oblivious to the lizard biting at her boot. Abeke thought Meilin had lost all sense until she spotted the masses of arrows being shot at her from all sides. Meilin's face was tight with concentration, unable to do anything but focus on keeping herself, and Jhi behind her, defended from the onslaught.

A badger flew at Abeke, stopped midair by Uraza.

Meilin needed help. Abeke looked desperately at the battlefield. Where was Rollan? Was he dead? And Maya?

"Abeke!" she heard Maya yell, as if in answer to her thought. Abeke spun to see the red-haired Euran still standing at the edge of the docks, eyes wide like she had seen a whole army of ghosts. She was pointing to Abeke's left with a terrified hand.

"GREENCLOAK FILTH!" Tahlia shouted, suddenly much closer and much less unconscious than Abeke had supposed. The Conqueror twitched her arm, and a knife flew straight and true into Abeke's shoulder.

For a moment, Abeke felt no pain, only rocked back by the force of the impact. She stared at the leather-wrapped hilt sticking out of her shoulder, stunned just long enough for Tahlia to kick a booted foot into Abeke's face. She fell back, and the impostor girl dropped roughly onto her chest and yanked the knife free. Then Abeke felt pain, and screamed.

"Louder!" Tahlia spat.

Uraza, apparently finished with the badger, pounced, knocking Tahlia off Abeke.

Abeke scrambled for her bow, but a heavy war hammer slammed down. Abeke rolled back in time, but the hammer shattered her bow.

She looked up into the face of a huge man, his brown hair tied in two braids. His face was covered with scars, and his mouth was a cruel grimace. He lifted his hammer and struck again. Abeke scrabbled over a crate and just missed getting crushed.

She heard Uraza's yowls, the calls of a leopard deep in a fight. Her cat could not come to her. Abeke pulled a dagger from her boot with her right hand. Her left shoulder stung with the knife wound, her left arm dangling. The braided man swung his hammer again. Abeke ducked, but he followed with a fist punch to the side of her head.

Her vision clouded and her head dropped to the ground, eyes facing the battle. She wished she had fallen looking the other way, because here she saw the dead and nearly dead. She saw Meilin turn to look at her, a moment of inattention that rewarded her with an arrow to her thigh. She saw Conor knocked from the back of Briggan, striking the wall of a nearby building hard, and slumping to the ground. She saw Briggan flicker, return to his natural size, and run limping, to Conor's side.

And in a huge mass, the Conqueror army swarmed forward.

There was a scream, and Abeke shuddered. She had hoped when the time came for her to die, she would do it with dignity. But the scream was one of mad lunatic fear, an animal scream. This was not the way she wished to end. Abeke pressed her lips together to stop the shriek, and found they were shut already. The scream was not hers.

"STOP IT!" the voice yelled.

By now that war hammer should have struck again, ending Abeke. She opened eyes that she had screwed shut and saw the soldier's braids blacken, turn into ash, and blow away in the wind.

"STOP IT!" came the voice again.

The soldier's face screwed up in a grimace of pain, raising his arms in an attempt to protect himself from an onslaught of heat. His sleeves started to char, catching fire like a log in a campfire. Abeke struggled to turn her head away from the sight.

"STOP IT!" the voice shrieked, and Abeke spotted Maya on the docks, eyes wide, lips pulled back to bare clenched teeth, her hand a rigid claw held high above her head. A wave of heat like a desert storm rolled across the dockside, the pulse of white light burning into Abeke's vision. Abeke held her arms in front of her head and opened her mouth to shout but the air in her lungs was pulled from her in a hot gasp. She felt like she had looked into the face of the sun on a midsummer's day, and the sun had looked back and screamed.

Then, as suddenly as it had come, the wave was gone. Maya lowered her arms and blinked. Everything was on fire. People, animals, buildings, crates. Conquerors ran in circles or toward the water, covered in flames, screaming. Abeke slapped at her clothing, hoping to douse flames that she soon found were not there. She drew back her hands, now smeared with a greasy, gray ash. She stood, and something thumped off her belly and onto the ground. It was the steel head of the war hammer – the wooden shaft burned away – covered in the same greasy ash that covered Abeke. Ash, she now realized, that had once been a braided soldier.

17

THE BILE

THE DOCKS WERE AFLAME. FOR A MOMENT, ROLLAN THOUGHT the Conquerors had unleashed mythological fire demons upon them, as the flames danced and ran like men. Then he realized they were men. On fire. Many were running haphazardly to the shore, some rolling on the ground. Others, those that appeared not to be actively on fire, were running the other direction, away from the docks and the battle.

Rollan scanned the scene desperately for his friends and found them unburned, small islands in a sea of flame. Conor, mouth agape, watched a fiery shape plunge into the sea. Meilin, covered in ash, held a blackened arrow, tip still flaming, staring at it like a confused wizard holding an unfamiliar wand. Abeke was slumped against the only crates not on fire, her hand covering a bleeding shoulder. She was staring at the dock, where Maya was kneeling, as if she had collapsed. Her head was down, her whole body slumped except for her right arm, extended palm up in front of her. It was like an invisible force was holding that arm, keeping her from falling.

A figure emerged from the water. Shane. He was burned and bedraggled, but very much alive.

"FORM UP!" he shouted.

A few others pulled themselves upright, and Rollan noticed several heads appear on the rooftops. Far fewer than there had been before. But still many more than the five Greencloaks.

"Come on, Rollan," Aidana said, suddenly behind him.

"I need to help my friends," he said.

"No, you don't. Not by running into the fray and getting killed."

She grabbed his wrist and pulled him, running.

"What was that!?" he gasped, slowing his pace.

"The docks are on fire," his mother said. "We keep moving."

"Did you know this was going to happen? Did your people set off a . . . a . . . fire bomb or something?"

"Don't be ridiculous," she said.

Rollan opened his mouth to speak, but Aidana squeezed his hand and looked in his eyes. "I only knew there would be a fight, and that it would turn ugly, and that your friends' side would have no chance. I didn't want you there."

Essix was nowhere to be seen, but Rollan knew she was telling the truth. People from the town pushed past them, running toward the blaze. They were carrying buckets. He stared at the flickering bit of dock he could see, mesmerized.

"We should go help," he muttered. He felt strangely

numb, as if he were just a boy in the audience of a town-square trouper show, just watching, unable to take part.

"The townspeople will help," Aidana said. "The Greencloaks must have caused it. They bring destruction wherever they go."

Destruction, like an ice palace in ruins.

"My friends . . ." he mumbled.

"Your friends?" Aidana's voice broke. "I'm your *mother*, Rollan. Please, son, I need you. Your friends, they use you. The Greencloaks are a violent bunch, intent on ruling the world, and liars all. Someone in your party told the Devourer you had Suka's talisman and where you would cross back into Eura. All we had to do was wait."

"No. No! None of them would –"

"How else could we have been waiting for you?" said Aidana. "You can't trust them, but you can trust me. I'm your blood."

Rollan shook his head. He could find no words.

"Let's go, Rollan," she said. "Not with Shane, not with the Greencloaks, let's just go somewhere and be a family. Away from all this." Her voice broke at the end, and her chin trembled.

He nodded. The trouper show continued on behind him, with the battle and the burning, as far away as a dream. But his mother held his hand, and her hand was warm. Only she felt real. He started to follow her down the alley, away from the noise.

A cry from high above. Essix pierced the smoke-filled sky and streaked toward him. She landed on his shoulder and firmly clamped her talons onto him, steadying herself.

"It would seem Essix agrees," Aidana said.

With Essix on his shoulder, Rollan's head cleared. He blinked, looked again into his mother's eyes, and nearly stumbled backward. For just a moment, he swore her eyes changed. Her pupils narrowed, her irises lightened to the yellow of tarnished brass.

"Rollan, is there –"

"What happened to you?" he asked, his voice trembling. Essix squeezed his shoulder, and he thought he saw faint black lines ghost about his mother, streaming away from her head, hands, and feet. Rollan took a step back.

The smoky string drifting from Aidana's left hand pulsed, and her arm shot forward spasmodically, gripping Rollan's wrist.

"Let go!" he shouted and tugged his arm back. "What's the matter with you? Stop it!"

Aidana's arm flopped with his effort, like the slackened arm of a doll, but her grip was like a vise. He winced with the pain. Any more pressure and he was sure his bones would break.

"Please," she said, teeth clenched as if it were she feeling the pain, and then closed her eyes. He watched her brow furrow, and the black lines flickered. She let go, breathing heavily as if she'd just run a mile. "It's not what you think."

Essix shifted her weight and Rollan realized the black trails behind his mother were gone. He hadn't imagined them, had he? No, those snake eyes. He'd seen those eyes.

"Something more is going on. Something is clinging to you – inside you –"

Aidana shook her head despairingly.

"I didn't know," she said. "I only took the Bile to make the sickness go away. I wanted to be myself again. I wanted to be your *mother.*" Tears wobbled in her eyes. "But now I'm less myself than I've ever been. I do things . . ." Her head lowered, as if she didn't quite have the energy to hold it up any longer. "It's like I'm a passenger in my own body. Since taking the Bile, sometimes it . . . controls me."

The Bile.

It was like someone had taken a blindfold off of him that he didn't know he was wearing.

The Bile, he thought with revulsion. *The magical cure-all Bile!*

Rollan touched the spot where she'd gripped his wrist, marks of her fingernails still raw and red there.

"But you fought it," he said. The lines had flickered as she let go. "You can break the control. Just now, I saw you do it!"

She stared at him, a spark of hope in eyes otherwise empty of anything but despair. "I try. I really do. But it's so hard."

Rollan took his mother's hand and pulled her up. "You never had help before. But you do now."

A smile lit her face, and she leaned her face down to his until their foreheads touched.

"I love you, Rollan," she said.

They stood this way until a bright flash in Rollan's peripheral vision caught his attention. He tried to draw back, but found Aidana was holding so tightly he couldn't fully disengage.

"Mother," he started, and realized there was a whine in his voice that he had only ever heard from spoiled rich kids in carriages on the streets of Concorba. "You can let go now," he said, and then saw her face was frozen in something that looked a lot like fear.

She was shaking. Her whole body had locked up, and she seemed to expend vast amounts of energy just to open her mouth in a whisper.

"Run," she rasped, and as he watched, the pupils of her eyes enlarged, nearly overtaking her now-yellow irises. Her grip slackened, releasing him. He fell to the ground with the suddenness of it, and Essix flapped off his shoulder to avoid being toppled. Aidana was standing where she had been, frozen in place, slowly mouthing something he could not hear.

He stood, and Essix dropped back onto his shoulder. When she did so, he was almost blinded by the appearance of hundreds of streams of pulsing black light driving into his mother's back. Her arm slithered slowly into her cloak. Wikerus materialized and immediately flapped up to hover above his mother's head like a dark cloud.

"Mother!" he said. "You need to concentrate! You can–" he started, but was interrupted by her scream.

"Run!" she yelled and flung a knife at his face.

Essix seized Rollan's hair in her talons and tugged just enough for the knife to sail past his ear, but by then Aidana was on him. Her fingernails raked across his cheek, and he felt something hard slam into his ribs. Essix screeched, and her beak drew back a chunk of meat from the soft flesh of Aidana's hand.

Wikerus let out an enraged caw and took to the sky, Essix leaping to catch him in a clash of feathers. Rollan scrambled backward, gasping for breath. His mother advanced awkwardly, as if on borrowed legs, her hand dripping blood onto the street. Her snake eyes stared without any hint of emotion, her mouth frozen in a terrifying grimace. Her voice gurgled from her throat like a thing trying to remember how to speak. Forward she lurched.

Rollan tried to speak to her, managing only a wheezed cough, but by then she had leaped atop him. Her knee landed in his stomach, knocking out his breath and bending him in half, vomit rising in his throat. Her hands clamped around his neck. He gasped for air that would not come and clawed weakly at her hands. He could feel hot wetness running down onto his chest, soaking his tunic. Whether it was his blood or Aidana's, he couldn't tell. Her teeth were bared, her mouth foaming like a rabid dog's. But even so, as the edges of his vision grew dark, he could see tears falling from those inhuman yellow eyes.

Rollan's arms grew heavy and his brain fogged. He began to wonder why he was struggling so hard. His fingers loosened from the hands around his throat and his eyes rolled to the side. The building he lay beside was made all of gray stone, except for a small, high window, which was of redbrick. The mix of the colors reminded Rollan of how old meat drains of blood. He closed his eyes to sleep.

And then, air. Beautiful, smoke-stained and dust-ridden air. He could breathe! His mother had let go and rolled off of him. She was thrashing on the ground, batting at the mass of talons and feathers clamped to her head. Her blows grew weaker, and under such an attack, her eyes would not last long.

"Essix, stop!" he tried to yell, but it came out a rasped whisper. Even so, the falcon let go of Aidana's face and took flight. Aidana's body collapsed to the ground, shuddering. Her eyes had survived, but the rest of her head and neck were covered in deep cuts and scratches. One wound below her jaw was bleeding profusely. Her cloak lay crumpled in a heap near his feet, and Rollan grabbed it and pressed the mass to her wound.

"You're going to be okay," he said. "Once the bleeding stops, you're going to be okay."

His breathing was too shallow and his speech was too fast. His hands were shaking. A part of his brain knew he was in shock, knew he needed to stop and think, to figure out what he could do in a rational way, but nothing except what he was doing right now seemed possible, at least not until he felt the sharp prick of a knife's blade in his forearm.

Aidana was holding a throwing knife to his arm. Just holding it there. He pulled his arm back, and she dropped the knife, deliberately, onto the ground in front of him. Her mouth moved in silent words, her yellow eyes brightened from the color of tarnished brass to that of the heart of a flame.

"Rollan!" someone shouted. Meilin? He couldn't tell.

He leaned closer to his mother. He felt like he really needed to hear what she was trying to say.

Footsteps sounded behind him. "Rollan! Are you okay?" Conor. That was Conor.

He put his ear to Aidana's lips.

"Kill . . . me . . ." she whispered.

Rollan stumbled backward, slipped on the knife at his feet, and landed on his backside. She didn't stand, just shook violently, as if her every muscle was working hard to keep from attacking again. Her eyes flickered yellow, pupils dilating again, and her gaze darted to where the weapon lay.

"Can you run?" Conor was asking. "We need to go. I mean, really, really need to go."

Rollan felt himself being pulled, first to his feet, and then away from his mother. Rollan stared at her as he went. He saw her eyes close, and he thought maybe that was it, that was the right thing to do, and he closed his too. His head felt light and wobbly, his body as distant as the sounds of battle. He tripped and fell, deciding that a nap right now made a lot of sense, except that someone was slapping his face. He opened his eyes and felt hands on either side of his face.

"Rollan! Rollan!"

Meilin. She was holding his face. That seemed sweet. She was right in front of him, her face in his. It was like a painting, a portrait of Meilin in front of a furry black-and-white flag. No. Not a flag. Jhi. He looked up and their eyes connected. Some of the smoke in his brain cleared.

"Rollan! Look at me!" Meilin shouted. He blinked. She pointed toward the shore, where a boat was casting off amid burned timber. "That is a boat," she said and turned his face back to hers. They were inches away from each other. He thought he liked that. "We need to get to that boat. Now." And then she slapped him again.

He stood up and stumbled after her.

Rollan was vaguely aware of things flying past his head as he ran. Arrows? He was running down the pier behind Conor and Meilin, the only one not completely demolished by fire. A few people waved encouragingly from the boat. Something stung him in the calf, and he stumbled but kept going. He was running out of pier. He saw Conor, Briggan, Abeke, Maya, and Tarik in the boat. Meilin jumped in. She turned to look at him. He was at least four feet from the edge of the pier and the boat was four feet beyond that, and increasing. No way could he jump more than eight feet, not without the Granite Ram.

"Run!" someone yelled from the boat. Maybe several people.

Someone else shouted "Jump," and so he did, realizing in mid-leap that the person who had shouted had been himself. He flew through the air, reaching out, but knowing he was too far to make it. As he braced himself for a plunge into the cold sea, something caught him. Something invisible. It felt like he was sitting on a cushion of air and was being drawn to the boat. He saw Meilin's hands outstretched, palms upward, her face screwed up in concentration. The crystal talisman around her neck was glowing. She had caught him.

Rollan readied himself to tumble onto the boat when something knocked him from Meilin's talisman-enhanced "hands," slamming him into the ocean. Freezing water stung his nose. He gurgled and struggled, fighting his way to the surface.

He gasped for breath, and Tarik and Meilin were there, reaching in the water to pull him out. Their hands were on his wrists when a second attack knocked the air out of him.

He went under again.

He clawed his way up, but the boat was moving away. Meilin reached out, yelling for him to "Swim, swim!"

He thrashed in the water and suddenly felt a tug upward. Meilin's ghost grasp had hold of his shoulders and was pulling him out and toward the boat. He was nearly there when Wikerus sliced through the air at Meilin, grasping at the Crystal Polar Bear with his feet. Meilin screamed, and Rollan dropped back into the icy waters.

Essix dove down with a screech, talons out, going for the raven's eyes. The raven let go of the talisman and flew away, but it had done its damage. The cord around Meilin's neck was cut, and the Crystal Polar Bear slid from her neck and into the waters below.

Rollan dove, aiming himself at the sparkling crystal talisman as it fell. It didn't occur to him that he was freezing. That he was so tired from running and fighting and bleeding that he was just seconds from passing out and making those icy waters his grave. In a burst of instinct he simply knew it was the right thing to do, and that he would be just as miserable and empty in the cold air as in the cold water, so he might as well do the right thing.

He could see the bear falling, still faintly aglow. Everything seemed to slow – the talisman, his kicking legs, his fading thoughts. He stretched his arm, trying to grab the talisman before it was gone, just managing to catch hold of it with numb fingers. He held the crystal bear to him, his energy gone, his goal achieved. He closed his eyes. Perhaps now he could sleep.

A tremendous force slammed into Rollan, rocking his mind awake enough to clamp down on lungs about to take a deep breath of ocean. He flailed and felt his hand break the surface of the water. His head followed, and he gasped for air. The fog in his brain cleared enough for him to realize his hands were empty. The talisman was gone.

He started to go under again when hands reached him. The boat had rowed around, and Tarik and Meilin pulled him back in.

"No!" He coughed seawater, struggling to speak. "No, put me back! The talisman –"

"It's too late," said Tarik.

A huge, gray creature, like the Great Beast version of the horror dog of the Ardu, was swimming away from their boat. One of its elephantine tusks had hooked the Crystal Polar Bear. It swam to the far shore and leaped out of the water on its belly, offering the talisman to a man in a black hood. He took the talisman and held it up, showing it proudly to Shane and a couple dozen other Conquerors on the edge of the burned docks.

"No!" said Rollan. "No, no, no!"

He rose, trying to jump in after it, but Tarik held him fast.

"It's done, Rollan!" said Tarik. "Don't sacrifice your life for what's already lost!"

Rollan struggled, his eyes on the shore. The Conquerors gloated over the Crystal Polar Bear that he and his friends had fought so hard for. The great gray, tusked beast stared back with a face as sharp as a spear. And Aidana – his mother – watched him with her dark eyes. Her face was covered in scratches, blood dripping off her chin, down her neck. She lifted her hand as if she would –

Shane approached Aidana, putting a kind arm around her shoulder, and her hand dropped. The two of them watched the boat recede, sadly, their shoulders stooped, their heads bowed.

Suddenly Rollan was shuddering with sobs he didn't know had been building. He pushed his palms against his aching heart and sobbed.

Tarik's arms were still around him – not holding him back now. Just holding him. Tarik patted his back, pressed Rollan's head to his shoulder, not speaking.

When the sobs slowed, Rollan still kept his face hidden, afraid to see their faces, to know if his friends thought him weak, careless, foolish.

He wiped his face off with his scarf and sat down, Tarik sitting beside him.

"A walrus," Rollan whispered. "Wouldn't you know it'd be a walrus. I know for sure now. I *hate* walruses."

The other kids laughed, the sound honest and nervous and full of pain.

"Rollan, are you okay?" Conor asked. "That woman. She almost killed you."

Rollan just stared into the distance. So many things found and lost so quickly. He'd lost the talisman. He'd lost his mother – again. Had she wanted to come with him there at the end? But even if she did, she was under the Bile's control. Oh, the Conquerors touted it as a cure-all, but forgot to mention how at any moment anyone who drank the Bile could become the Devourer's puppet.

She said she'd gone back to that house in Concorba where she'd left him on the steps waiting for a miraculous family who never claimed him. She'd gone back for him. And he'd go back for her. Somehow. He *would* save her from the Bile's control, if the only way was killing the Devourer with his own hands.

Rollan rubbed his face. He wasn't crying anymore, but his eyes were hot and stinging.

"Something happened to you," Tarik said. "Something more than losing the talisman."

Rollan shook his head. He didn't want to speak.

"All this struggle and hardship must feel overwhelming," Tarik said. "I believe you have known more loss than I can imagine. Life is full of loss. I have learned that what matters is how we fill the hole that the loss leaves behind. The Devourer is a great hole. He tries to consume the world to fill his loss, but domination will not satisfy his hungering need for wholeness."

Rollan saw Meilin put a hand over her face to hide her anguish. Rollan's heart hurt even worse. Meilin would understand if he told her about Aidana. Conor too, he believed. Tarik would comfort him. Abeke would be silent but not judge him. With a start he realized he knew how they all would react. This was his crew now. This was beginning to be his family.

But he didn't feel capable yet of telling the story. The pain was still as fresh as an arrow just entering his heart.

"Use what you have lost," Tarik said. "Draw from it. Swing from that loss and each punch will have more power."

Rollan nodded, but he didn't feel much like punching. He slumped to the boat's deck, sitting with his knees pulled to his chest. Between the legs of everyone else standing, he saw another figure huddled directly opposite him. Maya. He almost didn't recognize her with her red hair burned almost completely away, a pink wound across one cheek. The normally lively blue eyes were vacant. He couldn't tell if she was looking at him or not.

"The fire," he whispered. "It was her."

Conor dropped to one knee beside him. "She saved us. There were a hundred Conquerors, more maybe, each with a spirit animal. After Maya . . . blew up . . ." Conor paused, his eyes clouding with some memory Rollan did not have. "After that, a large part of their army was just gone."

Rollan saw Abeke sit down next to Maya and take her hand, saying something to her as Maya continued to stare forward.

"A hundred or more . . ." Rollan pressed shut his eyes. "The Conquerors were serious about this."

"And prepared enough to know we were coming," Conor said. He was looking at Meilin, who was holding Jhi's paw in an affectionate way that Rollan had never seen her do before, as Jhi licked at a wound on Meilin's leg. Everyone looked pretty beat up. Burns, bloodstained clothes, horror still in their eyes. He lifted a hand to his neck, felt the tender bruises forming there, shaped like his mother's fingers.

Tears began to well up, and a part of him wondered if all that seawater he'd swallowed trying not to drown was streaming out of his eyes.

Maya's empty eyes found his. Maybe it would be better to be burned out from the inside, he thought. To be emptied of thought and feeling and be as alone on the inside as he was in the world. He closed his eyes. Numbness. The invitation was alluring, the promise of never feeling again. Death might feel as welcoming as a warm bed.

Jhi left Meilin and ambled over to Maya, who looked at the panda, a little hope in her eyes. Jhi pressed her forehead against Maya's, and the girl's eyelids flickered, closed. Her body collapsed into slumber, her face at peace.

But Rollan's limbs trembled, rejecting the lure of sleep and forgetfulness. Jhi looked at him with her peaceful silver eyes, and Rollan shook his head. Even though he chose to stay awake and ache with the memory of all that had happened, as if the pain would keep his mother alive and well, he didn't know how much more he could bear. His heart felt ripped to tatters, his body beat up and abandoned.

A sudden weight on his forearm, a prickly grip on his skin. Essix looked at him with an unblinking eye. He wasn't ready to tell the others, but Essix knew. She knew about Aidana and her raven, she knew how Rollan's heart had been ripped, half-mended, and then ripped again. She knew what he did, what he said, and of those things left unspoken – all the details of the broken mess of his whole self. And still she hadn't abandoned him.

The cold wind picked up, ruffling her brownish gold feathers.

Rollan loosened the neck of his coat, exposing the skin. He lifted his chin – an invitation.

Essix leaned in and became a mark over his heart.

Shannon Hale is the *New York Times* bestselling author of *The Goose Girl*, *Rapunzel's Revenge*, *Ever After High*, *Dangerous*, and Newbery Honor winner *Princess Academy*. Her past pets include rabbits, birds, dogs, cats, lizards, and a snake who broke the world record for longevity. Currently her pets include four small children. She can be found herding them with her husband, author Dean Hale, somewhere in Utah.

Visit her website at shannonhale.com.